W9-CHI-263

A BIRD'S EYE

A BIRD'S EYE

CARY FAGAN

ANANSI

This edition published in 2013 by
House of Anansi Press Inc.
110 Spadina Avenue, Suite 801
Toronto, ON, M5V 2K4
Tel. 416-363-4343
Fax 416-363-1017
www.houseofanansi.com

Distributed in Canada by
HarperCollins Canada Ltd.
1995 Markham Road
Scarborough, ON, M1B 5M8
Toll free tel. 1-800-387-0117

House of Anansi Press is committed to protecting our natural environment. As part of our efforts, the interior of this book is printed on paper that contains 100% post-consumer recycled fibres, is acid-free, and is processed chlorine-free.

17 16 15 14 13   1 2 3 4 5

Library and Archives Canada Cataloguing in Publication

Fagan, Cary, author
    A bird's eye / Cary Fagan.

Issued in print and electronic formats.
ISBN 978-1-77089-310-8 (bound).—ISBN 978-1-77089-311-5
(html)

    I. Title.

PS8561.A375B57 2013   C813'.54   C2013-902796-3
                                       C2013-902797-1

Cover design: Brian Morgan
Text design and typesetting: Alysia Shewchuk

Canada Council   Conseil des Arts   ONTARIO ARTS COUNCIL
for the Arts   du Canada   CONSEIL DES ARTS DE L'ONTARIO

*We acknowledge for their financial support of our publishing program
the Canada Council for the Arts, the Ontario Arts Council, and the Government
of Canada through the Canada Book Fund.*

Printed and bound in Canada

FSC
www.fsc.org
MIX
Paper from
responsible sources
FSC® C016245

In memory of Michael Hersco

ONE

BIRTHMARK

My mother was born in a village infested with flies and smelling of donkey shit. It was a day's walk from Naples. This was 1901. She was born on the bare ground, nobody having the sense to bring a woman in labour inside while she could still walk; this, at least, is what my mother told me, but of course she felt only bitterness towards the place. Around her stood my grandmother's useless husband, her oldest sister, and a girl who was going to become a midwife but hadn't begun her training and wailed the whole time.

As soon as she was born, they saw it. On her tiny face a birthmark. Pale at birth but darkening over time, the birthmark had the exact shape of a handprint——forefinger reaching the right eye, thumb just behind the ear, pinky near the lip. She grew into a pretty young woman otherwise, fine featured, with full breasts and hips and a narrow waist, dark eyes. But all anybody in that village saw was her birthmark. They said that it was a clear sign, although they argued about what it meant. Some believed it proved that her mother had been a whore, others that the devil had disguised himself one night and was the true father, still others that a spirit or ghost lived inside her and would one day push out, splitting her skin from head to foot. All they agreed on was that she was defiled.

To this day I hate all villages and small towns anywhere for their closed-mindedness and collective stupidity. Give me a city, no matter how infested with con artists and the broken-hearted and the obscenely rich. The villagers took to calling her the Dark One. They did not let their own children play or even speak with her. She could not go to school, for her mere presence was declared disruptive. Her two older sisters resented her for stigmatizing them, and made her their servant from the youngest age. Her father hated being a figure of pity, which was a good-enough reason for him to beat her. The only one who loved her was her mother, and she died early of the influenza.

My grandfather blamed my mother for bringing bad luck on the family. But after his wife died, he did stop beating her. So my grandmother died for something, I suppose.

2

MOTHER MAKES A VOYAGE

My mother's name was Bella, named by her mother to protect her, which of course it never did. Human beings are unsophisticated in the way they take first impressions of people, and it was because of that birthmark that my grandfather made the decision to leave Italy. *How can I find her a husband when she looks as if another man's hand has already been upon her?* They left for America to find Bella a husband and grow rich.

But they did not go to America. They went to Canada because — my mother said — her ignorant father thought that Toronto was in New York State. In 1919 there were not so many Italians in Toronto, and they lived in narrow

5

houses, often several families in each. On College Street my grandfather opened a green-grocer's. Here Bella's sisters met the men who would marry them, here they brought their newborns in to weigh on the store scale. Her father married again, choosing a woman only ten years older than Bella. Bella herself was made to stand at the cash register from morning to evening, conveniently taking the money while displaying herself for sale. She might as well have had a price chalked on her.

Bella's solace was the motion pictures. She went every Saturday afternoon, insisting on having this time to herself. She didn't mind comedies, but she never laughed like the others in the audience. She preferred romances and, even more, weepies. These were romances with tragic endings. Lovers who missed their meetings at train stations. Children torn from their parents. Women who became mortally ill with unnamed sicknesses that left them increasingly weak but still beautiful. She brought two or three handkerchiefs with her and sat at the back and shook silently as the tears soaked her face.

The pictures were why, on the night of August 23, 1924, she decided to kill herself.

My mother was twenty-three years old. An old maid, an embarrassment to the family but at the same time a useful servant to her father, her sisters, and their children. She had gone to the Tivoli to see Buster Keaton in *The Navigator* but, coming out again unsatisfied, walked around the corner to Loew's. Slipping into the darkened theatre after the credits, she did not realize that the film — *A Woman of Paris* — had been written and directed by Charlie Chaplin, the first film that he did not star in. Nor did she know that audiences, wanting the Little Tramp, stayed away from his attempt at serious drama, and that the picture was already a flop. She avoided reading movie magazines for she did not want to know about the private lives of actors or the artifice of motion pictures. She hungered to fall into them as if they were more real than her own life.

She saw only that the theatre was almost empty, which suited her. She sat near the back, in the comforting darkness, the only place where she was ever truly happy, and let herself be enthralled. The film is the story of a young woman from a small village who moves to Paris and takes up a luxurious existence as the mistress of a businessman. But a second man loves her also, an artist from her village who follows her to Paris to woo her back. Bella gaped at the waste of two men wanting the same woman, but she didn't doubt whose love was the more true. Her hand went up to her mouth when the broken-hearted artist put a pistol to his breast.

At that moment, she became the man who could no longer live. She who was already dying inside, she who had never known a lover's kiss. And surely there was no living without love. Better to die quickly like the artist rather than in her own slow and agonizing way, trying to get through each hour, each day.

Bella watched the picture to the end and stayed for a second showing. At last she emerged from the theatre. Night had fallen and the lights burned up and down Yonge Street. She felt drops of rain, but they did not prevent her from walking purposely south, towards the docks. It began to pour.

At the ferry wharf, she bought a ticket to the Island. The ticket seller warned her that the boat would make one last return for the night. She managed to say that she only wanted to take the air and would not even be disembarking.

Standing at the rail, she tried to make herself

go into the water. The rain was stopping and the lake looked so black. Before she could work up her resolve, the Island dock approached. She waited as the ferry jarred against the old rubber tires and the metal gangplank cranked down. The rain had kept people away or sent them home early. Only one bedraggled figure in a drooping hat got on. Fortunately, he took up a position near the back.

The gangplank cranked up again and the ferry chugged out into the water. She waited for the Island to disappear in the darkness. The rain was all but over, but the lake looked even darker and more chilling. It took a terrible force of will to place the worn heel of her shoe on the first metal rung. She lifted her other leg; bile burned her throat. Her long skirt caught on a screw and she had to tear it free. She sobbed.

And what of me, her son? Do I wish for her to die, and for myself never to have been born? I want to say yes, for both of us, but I cannot. For what I've seen and done, what I've known, I cannot wish had been never. And she — surely even she, my tragic mother, would know her moments of joy. No, I say. Let her live.

3

MECHANICAL FISH

The man who heard her cry was named Jacob Kleeman. His own clothes were drenched and, being gaunt-faced and bony-limbed, with little flesh on him to keep in the heat even in August, he shivered while his crooked teeth chattered. Yet he was determined to test his new mechanical toy. A fish, nine inches long and made of several articulated tin sections plus the head and hinged fins. Wound up with a key and attached to a rod and short line, it was supposed to act like a real fish that had been hooked.

It had worked well enough in the bathwater at home, pulling and darting, although instead of leaping it had only thrashed at the surface.

Now he needed to test it in moving water. Always fearful and suspicious that somebody would steal his inventions, he had waited for a night without crowds. But the rain had been too heavy on the trip out.

The ferry was travelling faster than was ideal, but now that the rain had finally let up, he was impatient to try. He wound the spring mechanism with the key, which he then slipped into his pocket. He dangled the fish from the line where it wriggled fiercely, giving off a high *whirr*. He lowered it into the water and it immediately battered itself against the hull of the boat. For an anxious moment he lost sight of it, and when he pulled it up again, the fish spasmodic, he saw that several segments were dented and the tail fin had broken off.

Twelve weeks of work, hours spent every night no matter how exhausted, for this broken and useless thing.

He sighed, untied it from the rod, and slipped it inside his jacket.

And then he heard her.

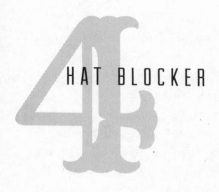

HAT BLOCKER

He had made the journey to Toronto because of his brother, Hayim. *Together,* Hayim had written, *with your genius for invention and my talent for selling, we shall become rich and happy.*

Jacob worked in the small family hotel in Otwock, a resort town on the Vistula. They all worked, from the oldest to the youngest, serving meals, washing laundry, fixing blocked toilets. The clientele, their suppliers, and their neighbours were Jews. They dealt with Gentiles only when paying taxes and bribing officials to keep their sons out of the army. They were religious but not scholarly, and they had made Hayim ambitious but without possibilities, and so he had broken their hearts by emigrating.

For Jacob, it wasn't so bad a life in Otwock. In his spare time he worked on his little mechanical projects. But his brother, my uncle, wrote to him from this place called Toronto that nobody had ever heard of. He described his spacious apartment, the good pay he received for satisfying work, the ease of starting a business of one's own. He wrote of the shops full of sparkling goods, the well-dressed women with narrow ankles. *Here*, he wrote, *everyone is treated the same, with dignity.* He lied because he needed Jacob. But he didn't lie when he wrote that the future was in the new country and that the old country was a graveyard.

So Jacob Kleeman used his savings and borrowed from relatives and paid for his fare. The five days aboard ship were horrendous, waves rolling ceaselessly, groans from every dark corner, the deck slurry with vomit. He arrived in Halifax half dead, and after the authorities checked him for lice and tuberculosis and infectious eye disease, he entered a world in which he could not understand a single word. Somehow he managed to buy a train ticket to Toronto, three days surviving on an apple and a hunk of bread, and when he finally stepped off the train at the old station in Toronto, he collapsed into his brother's arms.

Hayim had a second-floor room in a painted brick house on Euclid Avenue that leaned to one side. He shared it with a Litvak who played the violin but discovered that nobody wanted the old freylekhs and bulgars and had gone to work in a button factory. Jacob had not even a day before starting the job that Hayim had arranged for him, as a hat blocker in the Darling Building. The work made him ache for the freedom he had known in Otwock, and the amount of time he had once spent working outdoors and on his own interests. That he had once considered himself different from others and even superior, and had been made to feel that way by his own mother. who had called him her "little genius," worsened the day-by-day deepening of his gloom.

Only his nights of tinkering gave him any relief. Hayim said that he was too impractical, that he had no understanding of ordinary people and what they might want. His mechanical creations were too complicated or expensive to produce in quantity. They were striking and odd but not really pleasing. A lion tamer who bent over to put his head in a lion's mouth and straightened up again without it. A woman who gave a peanut to a monkey who then pulled off her dress.

Jacob's one practical design was for a simple and less expensive reservoir pen, a sketch that he had dashed off while eating his lunch at work when his own pen leaked. Hayim thought it might be what they were looking for, but Jacob refused to contribute his own year of savings, which was almost as much as Hayim had accumulated in five. He didn't trust an idea that came to him in less than a minute and, in any case, he didn't want his genius to be made known to the world by the introduction of a cheap pen. He wanted to present to the world something truly original, something brilliant.

Possibly my father really was a genius. His toys were as mechanically innovative as they were unsettling. He had a strange and haunted mind.

I AM CONCEIVED

She was so wet from the rain that his first impression was that of a woman climbing *onto* the ferry. But then she pulled her skirt free and he saw her leg begin to rise over the rail. He understood everything. Her agonized profile in the dark was beautiful and tragic, and my father, whose thoughts were always inward and who rarely noticed the faces of others, grew panicky with heroic purpose. Pigeon-toed, he ran to her.

She beat him with her hands as he pulled her back down, knocking off his battered hat, which spiralled over the rail. Then she collapsed, sobbing, in his arms. And he wept with her, his own pent-up grief suddenly released.

Between gasps, he spoke to her in Yiddish, one moment soothingly and the next barking with anger. She responded in the dialect of her village. They did not let go of each other until the ferry clanged against the wharf, when they moved down the gangway, his arm supporting her waist.

Each assumed the other to be a greener, just off the boat and without English. They made their way past the dark warehouses and railway sidings until they came to a small lot where a leaking feather mattress lay on a mound of corrugated iron. They fell together with a hunger that neither of them had ever felt so intensely, although neither was a virgin. (My mother had lost hers to a supplier of garlic and spices, who took her in the storage room, his hand pushing away the birthmark side of her face. My father was led by his brother to a brothel on Richmond Street where a French-Canadian woman with grown children was kind to him, although afterwards he threw up in the alley.) They pulled off layers of mended clothing, kissed and bit, pulled and grabbed. Their moans were fragments of lost language rising into the air, heard distantly by a night watchman at a coal depot who paused in the lighting of his cigarette.

Afterwards, they put on their clothes, avoiding one another's eyes. He walked her in silence to her family house on Mansfield Street, not many blocks from the room he shared. Standing before the house, she felt the dampness between her legs. The house had a garden in front — lettuce, tomatoes, and that long green vegetable that Jacob knew was eaten by Italians. She looked up into his eyes and he saw her face clearly for the first time. In English he said, "You are beautiful." She hurried up the porch stairs, fumbling for her key. He saw the ladder running up the back of her right stocking and thought: *She is my only chance at happiness*. And she, now closing the door, thought exactly the same. They were both as wrong as they could be.

My mother lay awake in the smallest room in the house, barely big enough for her narrow bed. She had washed herself in the bathroom, standing in the cast-iron tub and flushing water up between her legs, but one of my father's energetic sperm had already aggressively nestled itself into my mother's descended egg, showing more determination than he ever would.

BROTHERS

My father and his brother looked nothing alike. Jacob had wiry black hair, an olive complexion, hooded eyes. He walked as if shackled at the ankles. My uncle Hayim was green-eyed, fair, short but graceful. His accent was much less pronounced. He flirted with shopgirls. He was ambitious, and burned with envy when he read in the *Yiddisher Zhurnal* of a Jew venturing north to open a jewellery store on St. Clair or a cutter going out on his own with a line of overcoats. When he came out of work to find the union pushers with their pamphlets, he shoved them aside. His own future was among the bosses.

On a Saturday night he liked to have a little

fun. A streetcar ride to the new Sunnyside Beach, where he might meet a girl. On this night he only watched a baseball game in the Harbord playground, watching Jewish boys who were born here and felt at ease as he never would be. Returning, he was surprised to find that Jacob wasn't at home. Jacob always worked on his toys and then went to bed early. Perhaps he had fallen asleep on a park bench and wouldn't wake up until a cop tapped him with his nightstick.

Without Jacob home, Hayim had a hard time settling down to sleep. The Litvak's snoring was getting on his nerves. It was ridiculous, how his older brother needed looking after; he couldn't even find his way home. And Hayim also had to take care of their sister, Hannah, who would likely never marry. Hannah shared an attic room with a girl who worked with her at Tip Top Tailors, but when he made something of himself, the first thing Hayim would do was get them a decent place to live.

My aunt Hannah had taken the steamship over with Hayim but had almost been forced back to Europe. She had been held for eight days because of her club foot and Hayim, speaking little English and so unable to argue on her behalf, had waited every day until she was released. Even when they were children, he had protected her from bullies and insults.

And how were they to get their own place? Hayim thought, leaning back on his own bed. Here Jacob was fiddling around with ridiculous toys when he had already come up with a perfectly good design for a low-cost pen with a die-stamped nib and the simplest internal reservoir and screw-suction system for taking up ink that Hayim had ever seen. A pen for secretaries, schoolteachers, housewives. Why did Jacob not see the beauty in its simplicity rather than in the complications of his little clockwork monsters? All it would take was a few hundred dollars to produce the first batch. Hayim had three hundred, but he needed Jacob's money too.

His own he kept in a bank, but Jacob insisted on putting his money in a tobacco tin under the mattress. Hayim looked over to make sure that Malevsky was still asleep and then reached over to pull out the tin. He opened the lid and drew out the pile of bills to count them. Jacob would never have come to Canada to earn this money if Hayim hadn't pestered him. He had even found Jacob his job. What was the point of money just sitting there, earning nothing?

In what way was Jacob's stubborn refusal fair to Hayim or their sister? Surely Hayim would do them all a service if he started the business going and then brought Jacob into it.

He put the empty tin back and stuffed the money into the bottom of his own drawer. His heart pounded in his chest. But he knew what he had to do. Tomorrow he would become a businessman. And one day his brother would thank him.

TWO

ROOM

My room was the smallest in the house, hardly big enough for more than the bed. A small window overlooked the trash heap in the back garden. Kneeling, I could see my mother coming up from the cellar steps, hands black with coal dust. A smudge on her forehead darker than the birthmark. Kids taunted me because of her mark and reluctantly I had to defend her honour. I usually lost.

It was October 1938, and I was fourteen years old. The windowpane had frost at the edges. I traced my name with a dirty fingernail. From downstairs came the slam of a door. My mother made so much noise, I always knew where she was in the house. My father made almost none, a shadow with no more weight than a single inhalation of breath. Right now he was no doubt at the kitchen table, waiting for his breakfast.

"Benjamin!" My mother calling. "If you don't come now, I throw your eggs in the garbage."

I finished buttoning my shirt, glancing idly at the row of toys on the one shelf above the bed. Monkey. Fish. Lion tamer. Bear on a chain. Child riding on a crocodile. I had always owned them. When I was younger, my father had demonstrated them to me (not allowing me to wind them myself), but they hadn't been touched for years. There was one, a mechanical bird, that he told me was supposed to be his finest creation. Like the others, it was made out of tin and other metals, but with eyes made of glass, dark eyes that looked as if they saw everything and nothing at the same time. It had the shape and colour of a crow but also something of the jay and swallow, an imaginary merging of types. Its wings, folded in repose against its body, were larger in proportion than an actual bird's, as was its long and pointed beak that somehow looked as if it were smiling. Inside it was a clockwork timing mechanism that set the wings flapping for one minute. Then the wings would halt, stretched out in a gliding position, to start up again a minute later. During the glide, a rush of air was supposed to enter an open slit under the tail and turn a miniature paddlewheel inside, ratcheting up the spring again. My father's idea was that the bird would stay up until the parts wore out, or it crashed into something, or the weather forced it down. As a child I had imagined it staying up for months and even years, flying over roofs and schoolyards and streetcar tracks and dance halls and dark alleys. And as it flew, my father told me, every so often its mouth would open and it would emit a screeching laugh. But it was the only one of his toys that he didn't wind up for me, that he had never allowed to come to "life." He was too afraid that it would drive itself into the ground, or hit a church steeple, or destroy itself in some other way. It was too beautiful to wreck, he said. Actually, as a young boy, I thought it was a little frightening, with those dark, fathomless eyes. Now, however, I hardly noticed it. I didn't care about any of them, and the skill that my father once had meant nothing to me.

I hurried out of my room, slid down the

banister, sprinted past the dim wallpaper curling at the bottom. My father was drinking his coffee and reading yesterday's newspaper, which he had picked up somewhere. There was a headline about the chancellor of Germany and a photograph of a crowd in a square.

"Can I have the funnies?"

"After I read them," he grunted.

My mother dropped our plates onto the table. "If they taste like rubber, I don't care. Take some toast."

"I want a cup of coffee."

"You're fourteen."

"Give the boy some coffee."

"Ah, he speaks! Almost never, but when he does, what words of wisdom spill out. You want coffee, Benjamin? Fine. And tonight you can have whisky. Now I have to go. The stall won't open without me." She wiped her hands on her apron as she pulled it off. "Benny, you make sure you go to school today. And Jacob, I am afraid to ask what you are going to do."

"So don't ask."

"Tell me."

"I'm going to read this newspaper."

"Out of work three months."

"You haven't heard? I'm not the only one."

"There is always work. A day here and there."

"Not suitable work for a man of my talents."

"You have no talents. I have been think-ing. We can take in another boarder. It will be more work for me, of course. Benjamin, ask Mr. Speisman for more hours after school."

"I already asked him. He said he has to cut back my hours."

"More good news."

"Hitler wants to kill us all," my father said, rattling the paper.

"With your help," said my mother, "we'll starve before he has a chance."

BLACKBOARD

School was a form of torture, devised by evil beings. I dreamed of being Buck Rogers, Flash Gordon, the Green Hornet. Or someone with special powers, like Superman. If I could have one special power, what would it be? Strength? Flight? Definitely invisibility. Invisibility would allow me to put thumbtacks on Miss Patrick's chair for her to sit her big ass on. It would let me sneak into Doreen Kessler's older sister's bedroom when she was changing and see her titties. I could slip in at suppertime and my parents would stare in amazement as the fork and knife floated in the air and the food disappeared from my plate.

I was restless, small, quick. Physically more

like my uncle Hayim, whom I knew even though I'd been forbidden even to speak with him. My father complained that I had *shpilkas*, ants in the pants. At school I could hardly keep my knees under my desk, my hands from playing with a pencil stub. I would close my fingers around the pencil and imagine that I could make it dematerialize like Mandrake the Magician. But my mind was more like my father's had once been, always devising, always imagining a better way.

I heard my name and looked up. Miss Patrick was staring impatiently at me.

"Benjamin, march up to the blackboard right now."

I made my chair screech as I pushed it back. Only Mandrake could save me.

FAITH

My father did not believe in anything anymore — not in himself, not in family, and certainly not in the deity to which his father had prayed so fervently as he rocked on his heels. But every so often he made me go to the small *shul* on Brunswick Avenue, whether for my sake or for his I did not know.

"I don't see why I have to go. It's just mumbo-jumbo."

He cuffed me on the side of my head. I shook it off, then dragged my foot, pretending it was broken. I spent most of my time doing what adults themselves had no faith in. Already I believed only what I could figure out about the world.

"Walk properly," my father said, giving me a shake. In his hand was the worn velvet bag. A woman leaned out a second-storey window, her breasts pressed to the side of the frame as she reached around to wipe the next glass. The *shul* was in a small house. Hebrew painted on the glass door. Inside was an old sour smell, a drone of voices. My father gave me a tallis and the two of us draped them around our necks, he muttering a prayer. We stood at the back and I watched the men sway, stoop-shouldered. I couldn't resist the strange effect of the chanting, how it turned these salesmen and shopkeepers into something that felt holy. What was it? The room, the atmosphere, the sound, the silk and the embroidered letters, the lighting. A powerful effect causing a certain trick of the heart, that's what caught my attention. And afterwards, I knew, they would once more turn back into salesmen and shopkeepers.

Last year a gang of Protestant toughs pelted us with eggs on our way home. My father didn't even chase them. In his case, he had been transformed back into a bum. That's how I saw him, as less than nothing.

10

THE MARKET

My mother wore wool gloves with the fingertips cut off, a man's heavy overcoat, a washed-out kerchief over her hair. She shooed a pigeon with a deformed foot away from the bin of buckwheat. She sold barley, rice, cornmeal, spices from large jars: cardamom, turmeric, paprika, their intense, dusty colours. She stood under the corrugated overhang while Vogel, the vegetable seller across the way, played Al Jolson on his Silvertone. Before that it was Eddie Cantor, Molly Picon, "Mischa, Jascha, Toscha, Sascha." Old records—Vogel hadn't bought anything new in years. By now the Jewish singers had chased the Italian melodies from her head. She hadn't spoken to her relatives since marrying my father. It was ten years since she had used her own savings to buy the stall, her husband growing even less reliable with time. For two years, until kindergarten, I had sat on a small wooden crate eating chickpeas and watching the world pass, believing that Nassau and Augusta streets were the crossroads of the world and that my mother was its queen.

Mr. Kober, age seventy-seven, came by. His wife's legs were no good. Bella poured kasha into a paper bag and he watched carefully as she weighed it. Counted out the pennies. Three months, a husband out of work. In almost a year Jacob had not touched her. As if she wanted him. Sometimes, when he was out late at one of his card games, she would make her own pleasure. Then say to herself, *Enough, cow, go to sleep.*

She took the pencil from behind her ear and printed on a flat paper bag:

ROOM AND BOARD
$8 Month
Nice Room, Good Meals

These days, maybe eight dollars was too much.

She crossed it out and wrote "six," then tacked the note above the bins.

I was too old to visit her at the stall anymore; I didn't want to be seen by any kid I knew. I still believed that there was some little hope for me. A lifeline might be thrown, from where I had no idea, but if I watched for it and was quick, I could maybe catch it.

LUCK

The icebox was stacked with bottles of beer, the kitchen table cleared, and an extra chair brought in from the neighbour's. Exhausted from standing all day in the cold, my mother refused to serve her husband's "friends" and had already retreated upstairs. But I was happy to run to the corner for peanuts or a Jersey bar, pick up the bottles, and empty the ashes out of the Blue Ribbon Coffee tin. At the end of the night I would get nickel or dime tips and the biggest winner would give me a quarter. Even then I was making a study of human behaviour, although I didn't know it. I merely thought that I liked to see the way the players—Bluestein or Levin or

Pearlmutter — gave themselves away with little twitches of their eyebrows or sideways looks or movements of their mouths.

The slap of cards, the mumbled raises and calls from mouths dangling cigarettes or, in Pearlmutter's case, clenching a cigar. When there was nothing to do, I would stand behind my father, leaning on the gas range. He was the smartest player but too cautious about risking his money.

"The boy will learn something from you yet," said Bluestein, nodding.

"The way his mother talks to me, no wonder I get no respect."

"You respect your father, don't you?" asked Pearlmutter. But I didn't answer, just watched my father rake in the pot.

But after an hour or so, his luck started to run against him. Cards nobody could win with. He tried to slow his losses until the better hands started coming. Once or twice he bluffed, but Pearlmutter was too dumb to fold. And then I saw it.

My father dealt the second card. He did it by drawing the top card slightly back, letting his other hand catch the edge of the card underneath. He saved the top card for himself, which he must have caught a glimpse of. Turned over his hand. Three kings.

Nobody else had noticed. Nobody else had been looking hard enough. I felt myself almost giddy with the excitement of his getting away with it. For the rest of the night I watched my father's every move. He didn't cheat often, maybe every three or four hands. He won pots just big enough to keep him a little ahead, a few dollars. There was an elegance to it, the small moves of the hand, shifting away the attention. It was the most impressive thing I'd ever seen my father do.

At eleven o'clock, the men got up, complaining about their luck, the weather, the news from Europe, the continuing lack of business. When the last of them had closed the door, my father came up to me and slapped me hard.

"What are you doing, staring at me like that all night?"

I didn't answer. I didn't even mind so much the hot sting of my cheek. Not staring — that was a lesson too.

THE CIVIL WAR

Most children have a need for friendship that drives them to all sorts of hypocrisy, pretending to like what they don't, laughing at what isn't funny, ingratiating themselves with those whose good opinion may influence others. But even then I felt none of that, no need to be embraced as one of the pack. Instead, I kept to myself. Sometimes I went to the library, the big branch with the high arched windows at Gladstone Avenue, where I would sit at a table and read from a book that I pulled off the shelf. I didn't like made-up stories much; I preferred books on electronics or weather, or else books of history about places I hadn't even heard of. I didn't have a library card or know how to get one, and somehow I didn't think the haughty-looking librarians would give me one anyway, so I never took a book out and so never did finish one.

But what I liked to do best was to walk the city streets, sometimes far from my own neighbourhood. One Sunday afternoon I trudged along the bottom of the Rosedale ravine, and came up between two great houses. I passed between them and onto a circular drive where a chauffeur was giving a long black Packard a shampoo. The chauffeur stared at me and it was as if I suddenly saw my own patched trousers that were too big for me, my scuffed shoes and dirty cap. I would have kept walking, but he stopped his sponging and said, "What are you doing here, Himey? Scram." So I stopped. And stared at him. And picked up a stone off the drive. And ran full tilt, dragging that stone along the other side of the Packard's shining paint before taking off down the road with the chauffeur screaming bloody murder.

I walked at night too, slipping out the front door after my parents were asleep or even going out the window, which was dangerous in the winter because of the ice. It sometimes seemed to me as if there were two cities, the one in daylight where people toiled at their jobs and went to the shops and watched their children in the parks, and the one after dark when a whole other species took over. Night people. Washing down the streets. Leaning their heads on tavern bars. Taking swings at each other. It was at night when you could see what the Depression meant, people who were hiding all day coming out and shuffling along, hoping for a handout, a free meal. Others would hop off the trains before they pulled into the station and look for one of the camps just outside the city. Once, I walked through the grassy oval of Queen's Park, just behind the red stone building where the politicians made their speeches, and saw a dozen men sleeping on the wooden floor of the concert bandstand with newspapers spread over them. I walked back home and found the two glass bottles of milk left by the dairyman, still cold and beaded. I took the foil top off one and drank it entirely, until there wasn't a drop left.

And then came the night when I wasn't careful. I had spent a part of the night walking along the high arch of Davenport Avenue, which marked the edge of an ancient glacier, as a teacher had once told us in about the only bit of information I'd ever learned in school about where I lived. I was on my way home and was cutting through a back alley with tottering wooden garages and scruffy back gardens on either side, when I got jumped.

I didn't see them until they were already pulling me to the ground, kicking my feet out from under me. Three of them, a year or two older than me, and none I recognized. Fists pounding me in the side, ringing my ear, cracking my mouth. I flailed out hard and caught one of them in the chin with the heel of my shoe, but then a blow to my stomach sucked the wind out of me and I couldn't even gasp, couldn't see for the tears and pain.

And then I was alone, lying on the dirty ground. My limbs didn't want to move. I tasted the salty blood in my mouth. My eyes closed.

I realized that the back of my head was lying in a shallow puddle. But I was still getting my breath back and stayed where I was.

"Are you dead or what?"

A girl's voice. I opened my eyes. And saw a Negro girl looking down at me.

"What?"

"I said, are you dead? I can call the undertaker if you are. They got fancy black feathers for the horses to wear."

"I don't think I can get up."

"Grab my hand."

It hurt in about twelve places as she hauled me up. I bent over, but I didn't retch. "So what did you do?" she said. "Steal something?"

"I didn't do anything."

"You're too scrawny. You ought to carry a blade."

"I don't know who you are. You don't go to my school. And you talk different."

"Because I come from Louisiana. My daddy come up for a railroad job. Only you don't say railroad here. You say *railway*, stupidest thing I ever heard. You have awful weather, too. Got any money? We could buy some smokes."

"There aren't any stores open in the middle of the night. And I don't have any money."

"Then what did I bother saving you for?"

"You didn't save me. They ran off."

"'Cause I peppered their ugly butts with rocks."

I was breathing better now and I stood up straighter and looked at her. She was taller than me, gangly, like she hadn't finished growing into herself. Round-faced and toothy. Not really pretty.

A wave of nausea came over me. "I think I might throw up after all."

"Well, don't splash on my good shoes. My daddy just brought them for me. They're from Philadelphia."

This was my introduction to Corinne Foster. She was the first coloured person I had ever met, and I could not stop stealing glances at her whenever we passed under a street lamp. We walked down Albany Avenue to Bloor Street and sat on the steps of Trinity United Church and watched a Weston Bakery van go slowly by. She had been in Toronto for six months, brought by her father after her mother's death in a store robbery so that she could stay with her aunt and uncle while her father was on the trains. Her father worked for Mr. Pullman. People said that Mr. Pullman didn't hire Negroes who were too light-skinned, he preferred them dark. Her father was dark, but her mother had been very light and probably had some white in her from before the Civil War. All of this she volunteered freely. She expected that when winter came she was going to freeze to death. They went every Sunday to a Negro church and she had her hair done by a lady in a Negro barbershop, but it was nothing like her old home, she said, where it was a whole coloured community, practically a coloured town.

I didn't know what civil war she was talking about, nor did I understand half of what came rushing out of Corinne Foster's mouth. She was a talker, but she seemed satisfied by my listening and not saying much in reply. It is possible that I fell in love with her that night.

13

MR. WHITAKER

My father had not spoken to his brother for years, or to his sister either. But I knew that my uncle Hayim had kept his promise to Hannah. He had bought for them a small, handsome house on Winchester Street, close to the mansions on Sherbourne. It was like my uncle to choose a street where Jews were not particularly welcome, and to enjoy the discomfited looks of his neighbours when he doffed his hat to greet them in a loud and excessively friendly voice. He was always dressed in the latest style, for he had an English tailor on Bay Street, which marked him as newly rich in a manner that he did not quite recognize.

The Kleeman factory was at the west end of

Adelaide Street. All the metalwork was done there, the casting and stamping, while the celluloid tubes were bought from another factory to be turned on lathes into barrels. Then came the assembly and finishing. While other makers produced pens in all sorts of colours and even patterns, Kleeman pens were only black, which Hayim believed would emphasize their practicality and economy. His office was on the ground floor, and in the first years Hannah had been the bookkeeper, having gone to secretarial school. But as the company prospered, he had insisted that she give up working.

She hated where they lived. She missed her old friends from the factory, whom Hayim forbade her to see. She often walked the few blocks to Allan Gardens, for she loved the warm, scented air and rare flowers in the Palm House, but she did not feel comfortable among the women and nannies and prettily dressed children. Nor could the beautiful if unfashionably long dresses that Hayim insisted she wear disguise her limp.

Not that Hannah wasn't grateful. Gratitude was her stock-in-trade; it was all she had to offer — to people who were kind to her, who overlooked her deformity, who protected her.

Most of all, to Hayim. She feared him a little, she did not enjoy his company, but nevertheless she doted on him. And after all, he had no wife yet to look after him. Did he eat sufficiently? Was he working too hard? Could he not put aside the anger he felt about one thing or another?

She liked me to visit. A year ago I had knocked on the door and a maid had answered. But hearing a boy's voice, Hannah had come to the door. She felt a terrible guilt about Jacob and so was happy to welcome me into her home. I came every couple of weeks, not for her sake but for my own. She always plied me with food and gave me a present—a new book, the few dollars in her purse, a pair of leather gloves.

Today she wore a new crepe gown. I tried to guess what it cost. We sat having tea and delicious small cakes that she had sent the maid out for when I arrived. At the window of the front parlour, she looked out to see that dusk was slipping into night. Even to a boy it was obvious how lonely she was and that she was glad for my company, asking me about school and friends and my mother and father, causing me to make up more lies than I could keep track of. She mostly talked about my uncle, who told her about the problems in manufacturing and supply, the difficulty of securing government orders without belonging to the right clubs, the impossibility of joining those clubs. Even so, the business was successful. *The Pen That Works* — that was what the newspaper advertisements said.

Aunt Hannah, as she asked me to call her, crossed the room to the phonograph and looked through the new stack that Hayim had brought home for her. She liked to play her new records for me; they were the one luxury that pleased her. She chose Fritz Kreisler playing Brahms's violin concerto, and as it came on she stood with her eyes closed and I watched how it transformed her, the way music could do that for some people. And right then the front door opened with a bang and she quickly lifted the needle.

Voices, laughter. "Hannah? Hannah, I want you to meet someone."

My aunt was never comfortable with strangers, but she especially hated when her brother brought home guests — business associates or, worse, men he met at one of the restaurants he frequented. I sat rigidly in my chair, for my uncle was not nearly so fond of my visits. Hayim came in with a tall man with orange hair parted in the middle and a slack, rubbery face.

"Hannah, why are you hiding in the corner? Ah, I see our nephew is also here. This is my good friend Tobias Whitaker. Tobias's family owns Whitaker's Stationery, one of the biggest suppliers to businesses in the city. Toby, my sister. And our nephew Benjamin."

She looked pained as the man approached. "A great pleasure, Miss Kleeman," he said, taking her hand.

"We're absolutely starving," said Hayim. "Have Bess get us some supper. We'll just have a little drink in the meantime."

"Of course," she said. I could see she did not want to walk in front of this man, but she lowered her head and passed by him, excessively conscious of her uneven gait. As she left the room, she heard the men laugh.

My uncle didn't have much choice but to offer me something to eat as well, which I would have accepted even if I'd been full, which I wasn't. In the dining room, he described Mr. Whitaker's lineage, how he was a third-generation graduate of St. Michael's College.

Mr. Whitaker had recently returned from Europe. The Depression had shaken most of the Americans out of Paris, he said, and all anyone did was talk about the possibility of war. Hayim exclaimed about the Whitaker family home on Beverley Street. "A Victorian mansion, but completely modernized. You ought to see it, Hannah. This is a log cabin in comparison."

"But this is very sweet," Mr. Whitaker said. "And to tell you the truth, our neighbourhood isn't what it once was. A nearby home has just been purchased and there is a rumour that it is going to be divided into apartments. I can't think of anything more grotesque."

Hayim said, "Do you know how many pens we shipped last month? Eighteen thousand."

Aunt Hannah looked at me and said, "We have Benjamin's father to thank for that."

Hayim didn't look happy, but he said, "Yes, our brother. I am the first to admit Jacob's genius. I wanted him to come in with me, but he refused. It was his loss, I'm afraid. But let's not ruin the evening's fun. What do you say, Hannah? We could push aside the furniture and you and Toby could dance. He knows all the latest dances. What is that new one, the Lambeth Walk?"

"You know that I don't dance," Hannah said.

"But it would be my pleasure," Mr. Whitaker said, and smiled. My aunt looked at me as if to ask me not to desert her. But I knew that I would leave as soon as we got up from the table.

14 RUSSIAN NOVEL

At this time I was beginning to consider my escape from the family home. I had, I think, about as much sympathy for both my mother and father as an adolescent boy could have. I knew even then that they had never fully embraced the New World, much as they had wanted to escape the Old. Nor had they found a new world in each other. But that did not much mitigate my burning desire to live just about anywhere else. But I had no savings, and while I considered asking my aunt, I had some of my father's stubborn pride and didn't want to succeed on my uncle's money.

In the meantime, I had to find other ways

to escape. Slipping out of the house after dark, I had to squeeze out of my small window, grab onto the brick sill next to my own, place a foot at the top of the window just below, and then shimmy down the shaking rainspout. My hands slipped and I fell the last few feet.

"Hey," Corinne said. She could get out of her house before I could and so was always waiting for me.

"Hey yourself," I said back. It was hard to see much but her eyes. "What you want to do?"

"I got a couple of hours before my daddy's supposed to be home. He's coming from the Rocky Mountains. We could go to the river, try to find change that fell out of people's pockets doing the hootchy-kootchy."

"We never found anything last time. I got a piece of Black Jack." I unwrapped it, bit it in two, and gave her the other half.

She worked it in her mouth. "Hope I don't break a tooth."

"That wouldn't matter. You got, like, ten extra teeth." This was my way of hiding the fact that I was always thinking about her face, her mouth, her small round breasts under her shirt.

"I do not," she said.

"And fangs. Like Dracula."

"Well, I wouldn't suck your blood. You'd taste bad."

By now we were already walking down Markham Street, past the small dark houses, a cat slinking in a doorway. The two of us could walk for hours. We'd grow tired, but still we'd keep going, along the Humber River on the west or the Don on the east, up to the streetcar barns where we would look through the windows to see the men with their sparking blowtorches doing repairs.

I said, "Let's go to your aunt and uncle's house, Corinne."

"Oh, shut up."

"Why not? You've been to my house."

"I haven't been *in* your house, have I?"

I didn't have a reply to that.

"You really want to meet my daddy? He won't like you óne bit. "

"You said he won't be home for a couple of hours. Anyway, I won't go in. It's just to see where you live, that's all."

"Why you so interested? Oh, all right. I don't mind. At least I won't have to listen to you go on about it."

She started walking quickly down Crawford, and with her long legs it was an effort for me to keep up. I smacked her on the back with the flat of my hand and started running, but she caught up in a minute and then we were running together. The only time we stopped was when a police car came sliding along the street and we ducked behind some trash cans.

We got down to King Street, passed Dufferin, and then down Cowan Street. From there I could see the tops of some of the higher buildings on the Exhibition grounds. Only when a train rattled by did I realize we were fifty yards or so from the tracks.

"That's our place," she said, pointing to a small bungalow set far back from the street. There was a light on in the porch and I could see a figure sitting there. I slowed down, but Corinne grabbed me by the sleeve and we kept going, right up the walk. He was a small man, shorter than Corinne and much darker-skinned, although otherwise she looked like him. He had close-cropped hair and wore eyeglasses and had on a well-worn corduroy jacket. He had a thick book in his hands, and as he got up he put it on the rail.

"Your aunt wanted me to go looking for you. But I said there's no point, I won't find you. So I've been waiting up instead, trying to decide if I'm greatly displeased or *extremely* displeased by your behaviour."

"I'm sorry, Daddy. What are you reading?"

"You're changing the subject."

"I'm not. You know I like the books you like."

"It's *War and Peace*. By a Russian. It's long, but it's good. Who's your friend?"

"His name's Benjamin."

"Do your folks know you're here, Benjamin?"

I didn't see any advantage in lying to him. "No, sir," I said.

"I don't know what this age is coming to, the way children don't listen to their elders anymore. You two hungry? Auntie baked an apple rhubarb pie."

"Yes, Daddy."

"Come on inside, then. And don't wake up your aunt or uncle."

Another train went by, making the porch tremble as I went up the stairs behind Corinne. Inside, the house had a very large, bare kitchen, but all the other rooms were small. Her father took a milk bottle out of the very old icebox and cut us generous slices of pie, and while we ate he asked us questions as if he was genuinely curious. The pie was tart and sweet both. It turned Corinne's mouth red, and mine too, I suppose.

15

BODY AND SOUL

With so many people needing to rent out rooms, boarders were not easy to find. Nevertheless, my mother turned down a woman just arrived from Port Arthur on the grounds that we already had a woman boarder and they were far more demanding than men. Three weeks went by before a man offered to take it, but my mother said that he was too feeble and that, if he died in bed, who would pay for the funeral?

At last came a third. His name was Sigismond Eisler. Totally bald but virile-looking and with the bushy eyebrows of a moving-pictures comedian. Full lips, a barrel chest, bowlegged. An unattractive man, but with a certain tenderness in his eyes — this is what Bella saw. His possessions were held in two suitcases tied with rope, which he carried uncomplainingly from the market to the house and up the stairs. He looked into the room for significantly longer than was needed to take it in.

"I am a good cook," Bella said.

"It is reminding me a little of my boyhood room. Yes, I will take it with gratitude."

He pressed the back of his hand to his forehead and closed his eyes a moment, as if a terrible image had come to him. She wanted to reach out and touch his hand, but she said, "You can pay rent today?"

"I have a wife and child."

"Here? The room is too small."

"In Germany. She refused to leave. We did not have the same political ideas. They will come for me if I stay. I was a coward to leave, perhaps."

She had never heard a man say such a thing about himself. But there is a kind of man who needs to prostrate himself even before strangers, eternally hoping for forgiveness. She watched him take out his shabby wallet and count out the money. She took the bills from his thick fingers and slipped them into the pocket of her apron.

"Dinner is in an hour," she said.

Of course, I did not see all this myself—there is much that I did not see directly. But just as it is possible to guess that a man is thinking of an ace or a heart, or that a woman in the audience wishing to volunteer will be pliant or troublesome, so it is possible to know what is said and done, what is desired and feared.

I did, however, see my mother ladle the *pasta al forno* from the ceramic dish onto the new boarder's plate. Miss Kussman passed it to him, not hiding her resentment at having been displaced one seat at the table. I watched the new boarder take up a forkful and put it experimentally into his mouth. His eyes bulged as he opened his mouth and fanned with his hand.

"It . . . is . . . hot!"

"Food should be hot. You like it?"

"It is very good."

My father snorted and, ignoring the knife, tore off the end of the bread. Miss Kussman said, "And what sort of work did you do back in Germany, if I may ask?" She herself worked in the Neilson's factory and sometimes brought me broken chocolate bars in a paper bag that I now shared with Corinne. She had a prominent Adam's apple that reminded me of Olive Oyl.

"I was working in the office of an archi-tect. Making models. Flats for working people. Common spaces. Gardens and meeting rooms. But then there was no work."

"And there's no work here," my father said.

"Yes, you are an expert on that," my moth-er said.

Miss Kussman asked, "And what are you doing now?"

"Oh, anything to keep body and soul togeth-er." He was digging into his food now, hardly able to eat fast enough. "Mr. Kleeman," he said. "You are not related to the Kleeman Writing Instrument Company? I see their advertise-ments everywhere. I even have one, you see?"

My mother laughed. She laughed again, flinging back her head, and the boarder looked up at her as if she might be a little mad.

COWTOWN

"When I grow up, I'm going to move to New York. Going to be a singer. A big star."

We were walking down Yonge Street on Saturday night, past Muirhead's Cafeteria, Scholes Hotel. Laughter from a tavern door as it opened, smell of beer and cigarettes. Women with cheap fur collars held on to their men.

"Why do you have to go to New York?" I said, not quite understanding my envy.

"You can't be a real singer in this town. Here they like the Andrews Sisters. Bing Crosby. All that smooth stuff. This is a cowtown."

"It isn't."

"Where's your coloured section? Where's

your Cotton Club? It isn't a big city without Negro people."

We stopped in front of Heintzman Hall and looked through the plate glass at the shining black pianos. I wondered whether she was right. In truth, the farthest I'd managed to imagine was leaving the house of my parents. It had never before that moment occurred to me that I might go somewhere else, and I felt almost as if the wind had been knocked out of me.

A sailor stumbled into me and kept going.

"Anyway," I said. "You can't be a famous singer. You've got a voice like a washing machine."

"Take that back."

She grabbed my arm and bent it behind my back. Grimacing, I tried to pull myself free, but she had me good. I squinted through the tears and saw the marquee for Brant's Vaudeville. *All Live! Shows Running Continuously Till Midnight.*

"I'll let you go if you come in with me," she said.

"But . . . we don't have . . . any . . . money."

"So? We'll sneak in. The doorman isn't even there. Probably on a piss break."

"We might get caught."

"Will you come with me or do I twist your arm a bit more?"

"Okay, okay."

Corinne let go, only to grab my sleeve. She pulled me down to sneak under the ticket booth and then rushed me through the door and across the red lobby carpet. She yanked open the inside door and then we were in the dark of the theatre. We stood letting our eyes adjust. A man with a dog act was on. Every time he bent over to pick something up, one of the dogs jumped on his back.

"Those dogs are smarter than you," she whispered. "Come on."

She skipped down the aisle and slid into a seat three rows from the front. I took the seat beside her. The man and the dogs took their bows and the curtain came down. Three girls came on and did a fake cancan.

"Those women are all so ugly they must be sisters."

True, but I looked at their frilly underpants anyway. After them came a violinist and an Irish singer, followed by a husband-and-wife comedy act. I was thinking about putting my hand onto Corinne's knobby knee, whether I'd get a slap to the head, when the curtain came up on a man in tails and top hat. He was drunk, or seemed it anyway, trying to keep himself upright as he patted his pockets in search of a cigarette. When he came up empty, he shrugged, but when he put his hand to his lips, a burning cigarette appeared. Surprised, he dropped it onto the stage and stamped it out. But another appeared in the same hand, and then a third in his other hand. He threw them down too, but more cigarettes replaced them and then one seemed to jump into his mouth. He staggered about in increasing dismay, burning cigarettes appearing faster than he could drop them.

The audience laughed, but I leaned forward, riveted. How did the cigarettes just appear? I hated the drunk act, the slurred voice, the cheap humour, but none of that mattered. Anyone could learn to dance, or tell a joke, but this man broke the laws of nature. He made a tear in the world and put his hand through it. I didn't know that he was one of a hundred imitators of Cardini, one of the greatest sleight-of-hand magicians of the time. I only knew that I too wanted to pull objects out of the air.

When we left the theatre, I couldn't talk. Corinne gabbed on about this or that act, but I had no words. Instead, I made her walk quickly up to College Street then past the market, up to deserted Harbord, and through the back alley into the back garden of my house. Most of the garden was taken up with an old, high shed where years ago my father had kept a horse. He had left the factory and for a year or two, while my uncle was beginning to make his fortune, had sold pots and kettles from a wagon. I had been three or four, but I could still remember that old sway-backed horse. Once, my father had let me feed it some carrot tops.

"What are you up to?" Corinne said when I pushed the shed door open and led her inside. It was dark but for slits of lamplight leaking in between some of the slats. Mouldering straw still lay on the dirt ground. Some rusted tools leaned in a corner. "I bet there are mice in here. Maybe spiders . . ."

I grabbed Corinne and kissed her. I didn't even know how to kiss; our teeth banged together. She started to push me away, her hands flat on my chest, but I pulled her tighter and pressed my pelvis against hers. My body was a fire of pain. "You can't . . . tell . . . anybody," she said, pulling off her shirt. She smelled of sweat and lemon soap. We stepped away from each other and, eyes down, took all our clothes off and laid them over the straw.

"Don't you think I ever did this before," she said.

"I don't."

"You're only fourteen."

"You're only sixteen."

"You don't have one of those rubber things."

"I do have one."

It hadn't been easy to get, but I had made the effort because I didn't think that Corinne would agree without it. Everyone knew there was a Parents' Information Bureau worker who would supply you as long as you didn't look like a cop. All I had to do was pay a guy who worked at one of the stalls to tell the woman he wanted it for himself and his wife. Now I pulled the package out of my pocket to show her.

"You mean you've been planning this?"

"I don't know how to use it exactly," I admitted.

"We can figure it out," she said.

I could not believe the softness of her skin. But we were both rough with each other, like children wrestling. That first time was more a relief than a pleasure. But there would be the next day and the day after that and the day after that. At other times we would talk just as we did before, as if nothing had changed. But there was something new between us. Something precious that would protect us.

17

LITTLE PICTURES

My mother did not have the needs of an adolescent but the hunger of someone who believed that her time was running out. If it hadn't been the German, then someone else? But it was the German.

So she put her ear to his door and listened. It was only nine o'clock, but perhaps he was already sleeping. He did keep unusual hours, sometimes going out at ten in the evening, sometimes not leaving the room at all.

His voice startled her. "Is someone there?"

She backed away. "It's only me. Mrs. Kleeman. Bella. I brought you a piece of cake and a cup of tea. But if you don't want it . . ."

The door opened. He stood in his undershirt

tucked into his trousers. "Yah, please come in. It is most kind of you."

Without his glasses, his face looked even rounder, his eyes smaller. He stepped aside to let her in. "Here I am two days with the rent late and you bring me cake. But I have half of it for you."

There was no table, so she put the oval tray on the dresser. He had rearranged the room, moving the bed against the wall to make a small space by the window for an artist's easel. She had never seen one before except in the movies, and it was almost exotic. Small jars of paint rested on a wooden stool spotted with colour.

"I see you have brought two cups. You will join me?"

"Yes. You're an artist?"

"No, no. Not at all. I just make little pictures and sell them. Down on the boardwalk by the lake, where people like to stroll on the weekends. Come and see if you like."

He led her to the other side of the easel. A board rested on it, divided into twenty small squares. Each square was a little painting in progress: a girl with a balloon by the Eiffel Tower, a dog asleep with the Colosseum in the background. The red and blue had been painted in all of them, but the rest was only sketched.

"They're so pretty."

"I have no imagination. I paint the same over and over. Children like them. Young men buy them for their sweethearts. They make the world small, like a story, a plaything."

"You have paint on your face," my mother said. And because she hungered for tenderness herself, she put the tip of her finger to her tongue and then touched his face.

"Bella." He held her hand there. With his own hand he reached up to touch her birthmark and then, his fingers caressing her neck, pull her close.

At dinner, a spot of paint on my mother's neck. She kept touching it with the tip of her finger.

18
PROFESSOR HOFFMANN

I wanted to know more about what the man in the tuxedo had done onstage, and the library was the only place I could think of to go, although I didn't feel optimistic. And although I believed that most, if not all, of human knowledge was contained within the walls of the Gladstone Library, I doubted that the sort of knowledge I sought could be found in books. Still, as soon as I thought of it, I headed to the library, not considering the fact that it was after dark and the place might be closed. And sure enough, I stood on Bloor Street and looked at the dark building, outlined by a spill of light from the gas station beside it. I was about to turn away when I noticed a single bulb above a side door, and at that same moment the door opened and a woman stepped out. She juggled a set of keys to lock up. Tall, in a cloth coat and a hat that looked too small for her head. *What would Corinne do?* is what I thought to myself before walking quickly up to her.

"Please, miss. I want a book."

She turned around and looked at me. She had a long, appealing face, like a horse. "I'm sorry. The library is closed until morning."

I must have looked crushed, because her face softened. "Do you have a library card?"

"No, miss."

"You look familiar. Have you been here before?"

"Sometimes."

"And no library card. All you have to do is have your mother and father come in. This is just the sort of hurdle we have to overcome with you immigrant families. Well, my evening engagement was cancelled anyway. It wouldn't hurt to go get some work cleared off my desk."

She put the key back in the lock and opened the door again, turning on a light. I followed her in through the back rooms, past coat racks and crowded desks and a battered lunch table, up the stairs and into the broad reading room. I was naive enough to believe that she must have read every book on the long rows of shelves.

"I think it best if we keep most of the lights off," she said. "We might draw the interest of the local constable and have to explain ourselves. Now, the card catalogue is right here if you haven't used it. What is the book you're looking for?" She took a flashlight from a desk.

"I don't know which one exactly." The truth was, I didn't know if there was such a book.

The librarian pointed the flashlight at me. "Can you tell me the subject?"

"Magic."

"You mean witches and sorcerers, that sort of thing?"

"I mean what a man does in the theatre. With cards and cigarettes and making things disappear."

"Conjuring. So that's what has brought you so urgently to the library. As good a subject as any. Let's look under the subject heading. You see here? We have just a few titles. Most are for children. I believe that Hoffmann's *Modern Magic* is the best, but it's hardly intended for someone your age."

"I want to see it, please."

"We'll just write down the Dewey number. And now to the books."

She swung the flashlight beam to the carpet and led us to the shelves. She leaned down and ran her finger along the spines until she pulled out a small, thick volume. Standing again, she put it in my hands. The author was listed as "Professor Hoffmann." The book fell open to a small picture, an engraving of a hand lifting up a pan to reveal flames rising from inside. I read the words underneath. *Borrowed rings and live dove produced from an omelet.*

"Can I take it home?"

"Unfortunately, it's a reference copy, which means that it doesn't circulate. You have to use it in the library. But I'll tell you what. I've got some work that I can do. You sit down and read for an hour. I can give you paper and a pencil if you want to make notes. And afterwards, I'll keep it at my desk and you can come in during regular hours. Would that do?"

"Yes, miss, thank you."

"And what is your name?"

"Benjamin."

"Very good, Benjamin. I am Miss Pensler. You sit over here. I think we can risk turning on one reading lamp."

At the desk, I turned one page after another. What I saw was too wonderful, and too much to take in.

19
A SMALL DRINK

My uncle's intention may not have been to keep his sister a prisoner in their home, but the effect didn't look much different to me. The visits of Tobias Whitaker, accompanying her brother home, were at least a break from the monotony of her days, but it wasn't as if she enjoyed them much. Mr. Whitaker was attentive to her, often bringing a box of chocolates or a bouquet or even the latest copy of *Picture Play* or *True Story*, which he supposed she might like. He looked pale as a china dish to me, whenever I saw him (Hannah slipping me the chocolates), like some kind of cold-blooded animal needing to borrow another creature's warmth.

One early evening, Mr. Whitaker appeared at the door. Hayim was still at the factory — he kept long hours — and she had dismissed the maid in order to be alone. She stood holding it open to the cold evening air. Here was Hayim's friend, weaving a little from drink and crumpling his handsome hat in his hand.

"I'm so sorry, Mr. Whitaker, but my brother is out."

"I've already been to see him. And now I've come to see you, if that's all right."

"Of course." She felt the flush of her cheeks. Her brother had always encouraged her to be friendly to Mr. Whitaker, and now he was coming to see her by himself. She ushered him into the sitting room, walking slowly so as to make her limp less noticeable. But it was his own nervousness that alarmed her, how he fiddled and looked anxiously about and licked his lips. She sat first and he perched across from her on a silk settee.

"The maid has gone out, but I could make some tea."

"Oh no, don't bother. Perhaps I could just take myself a small drink."

"Of course."

She watched as he went to the side table and

poured himself a glass of Seagram's. He drank it down and sat again.

"Forgive me, Miss Kleeman. Hannah. I have been trying all evening to fortify my courage, you might say. And now I must say what I've come for."

He stood up and startled her by immediately dropping to his knees, his hands flailing. She could see his red hair was thinning, which made her feel more warmly towards him. He reached up and grabbed her hands.

"Please, Mr. Whitaker."

"No, I won't let go. I've been captured by your sweetness, your goodness. These visits are the highlight of my days. I wake up each morning thinking of you."

"You're being horrible to me. I didn't think you were like that. When my brother gets home —"

"But he knows I'm here. He says that the difference in our faiths isn't a problem for him. He doesn't object to your conversion. My family has a good name, and that counts for something in this town. I want you to marry me, Hannah."

Her breaths came so quickly that she became almost faint. He had to support her arm.

To be the deepest concern of a man. To escape this house. To be loved. Tears stung her eyes and sobs convulsed her. She felt absolutely stupid, but she just couldn't stop.

20

JEALOUSY

Miss Pensler had told me to come during regular hours, but I would wait for her instead at the end of the day so that the two of us could have the library to ourselves. I think that it was already becoming my way, to operate in secrecy, in the shadows of near dark, and somewhere between the rules. Miss Pensler herself must have enjoyed our little conspiracy for, despite sighs and eye rolling, she always let us back in.

It says something about my feelings that, instead of keeping these visits always to my-self, I decided to bring Corinne with me. And Corinne was eager to go. She liked reading much more than me; I wasn't interested in any story but the one I was trying to write for myself. But really she wanted to come because she was suspicious of this Miss Pensler who didn't mind spending some of her free evening hours with me. "Just don't tell me that she's got literature on her mind," Corinne said, stretching out the word: *lit-a-ra-toor*. This jealousy by my sixteen-year-old lover made me uncomfortable and proud at the same time, and I didn't know if I should reassure her or encourage it, but in any case I was far too inexperienced to attempt either.

And so one evening Corinne trailed behind me, suddenly unsure, as I went up to the door just as Miss Pensler was coming out.

"I brought a friend with me," I said.

"Now Benjamin, you know the library has closed. Letting one person in is bending the rules enough. If Mr. Clare finds out, I could be dismissed."

"Who's Mr. Clare?"

"The head of the branch."

"Aren't you the head?"

"I certainly deserve to be. Well, come in, then, before somebody sees."

Corinne followed and I could feel her wariness even without looking back. We went through the workrooms to the stairs and up into the reading room.

"Go turn on the lamp and I'll get Professor Hoffmann for you."

After she left us, Corinne said, "I saw it."

"What?"

"In your hand. The coin. It caught the lamplight."

"Ah, damn."

"How long have you been doing it?"

"Maybe half an hour. Passing it back and forth."

"Pretty good. Anything else?"

She never asked to see what I had been practising and I suspected she was trying to get on my good side. But I opened my hand to show her the quarter. Then passed my other hand over it and the coin was gone. Corinne nodded solemnly.

Miss Pensler returned. "Here you go. We can't stay too long, I have an engagement this evening. Would your friend like something to read? I've got a lovely illustrated book of Aesop's fables just in. They're very short."

"I'm a good reader," Corinne said, sounding more herself. "I just read Daphne du Maurier, and before that Marjorie Kinnan Rawlings."

"I see. Then I'll point you to our latest fiction."

I watched them go off. Corinne looked back at me and stuck out her tongue.

21

COLOURED BEADS

I see my father walking home, not with his usual stroll but hunched over from a pulsing headache. Maybe it was from all the smoke in the back of the coffee shop on Dupont when he'd lost his last five dollars on dice. He stopped to look at a window display of artificial limbs and, in spite of the headache, roll himself a cigarette. He could never roll them as clean and tight as I used to do for him, and the thought of it made him aware for a moment of my frequent absences.

Maybe a nap would do him good. At least the house would be quiet in the afternoon, with Bella at the market and the tenants out. Maybe Herr Eisler wasn't what he said he was.

Maybe he was a spy in search of the mechanical inventions that existed only in Jacob's head.

When he reached the front porch, he noted the newspaper pages blown all over the porch but didn't pick them up. He unlocked the door, hung up his hat, and climbed the stairs.

If they had been listening, my mother and Mr. Eisler would surely have heard him, for every step squeaked or groaned. But they were breathing too hard, whispering in each other's ears, feeling the rise of their desire.

My father went into the bedroom, removed his shoes, and lay on his back with his hands on his stomach. He closed his eyes. The room smelled pleasantly of talc.

And opened them again. What was that stupid Kraut doing in his room? Calisthenics? He was making the wall shake; the light fixture's loops of coloured beads trembled. He heard a muffled word. A cry.

So the Kraut had a woman in there. Guests were against the rules, but still — the lucky bastard. Of course, she was probably old and ugly as sin.

My father closed his eyes again.

22

NOVELTY

To me it looked like a building that might be in London or New York, a stone arch entrance and two great plate-glass shop windows on either side, four storeys of more windows and roman pillars, and then three ornate pointed roofs. It was called an arcade because inside there were rows of shops. It was Miss Pensler who had told me about it, and at first I thought she was teasing me because such a place couldn't possibly exist. But here it was, with a window on Yonge Street straight across from Temperance Street, in large letters *Whitlam's Magic Tricks* on the sign across the top of the window and in smaller letters *Japanese Magic and Novelty Store*. I couldn't see in because there was a drape pulled with just some dusty paper lanterns hanging in front.

"Are we going in or not?" Corinne asked, impatient as usual. I hesitated still, feeling a loss of nerve, and so she opened the door and pushed me inside. It was a much smaller shop than the spectacular place I had imagined, narrow and with some party supplies — paper hats, balloons, that sort of thing — on otherwise bare shelves. A counter at the end with a brass cash register sitting on it. Three men, one behind the counter. The other two — fat and skinny like Laurel and Hardy — ignored us and went on talking.

"And that's how Leipzig came up with it."

"I hear he's on death's door."

"Probably started the rumour himself."

Corinne gave me another shove. I stumbled forward and then walked up to the counter. All three men turned to look at me. Although I hadn't known what to expect, I was surprised by their ordinariness, three men I wouldn't have noticed in a bus station or at a lunch counter. They didn't look hostile so much as vaguely curious, and the man behind the counter said "Yes?" and stroked his bald head as if he had a nervous tic.

"I want to buy a hand box."

"A hand box?"

"For vanishing a handkerchief."

The three men burst into laughter. "Yes, Joe," said the fat one, "I've just got to have a hand box too."

"And how about an egg bag while you're at it?" the skinny one said.

"I already made one."

More laughter. Corinne came up and yanked me by the back of my jacket. "Show them," she said.

I shushed her, but the fat one said, "Show us what?"

I took a deep breath. "Please bend down," I said.

"What's that?"

I motioned with my finger. The fat man bent over. "I guess this is why you couldn't hear me," I said, pulling an egg from his ear.

"Well, well," said the skinny man.

"Let me see that." The fat man snatched the egg from me. "Hey fellas, it's a real egg, not a shell. Good job, kid. That's a sizable item for your age. Joe, serve the gentleman."

"I certainly will. What's your name, son?"

"Benjamin Kleeman."

"Okay, Benjamin. First of all, I don't know what you've been reading. Erdnase? Hoffmann?"

"Both."

"Fine. But there's more recent material that's a lot easier to follow. Second, don't waste your money on a gimmick that's going to give you a twenty-second effect. Get something that you can really work up and that will improve your skills. You've got good hands, how about something classic? A nice set of chop cups."

He reached under the counter and brought out a set of silver cups and four small red balls made of rubber. "You can hold an audience for a good five, six minutes with a full routine. If you finish off with something like lemons, whammo, you've got them in the palm of your hand. Five bucks and I'll throw in the literature."

"Joe, you're giving something away?"

"Young talent has to be nurtured. I wouldn't want the art to die with the likes of you two."

I picked up the shining cups and held them in my hands. Real magician's props, the first I ever owned.

23

THE DIRECTORY

I f I didn't have deliveries to make for the drugstore and Corinne didn't have church choir, we would head for the shed as soon as we were sprung from school, dumping our books on the dirt floor and leaping at each other. We made love in the shed behind the house the way children play games, always changing the rules, insisting, refusing, sulking, laughing. Finding ourselves unable to stop, no matter how sore or satiated. We would lose all track of time and then I would hear my mother calling for supper and we would hastily put our clothes back on. Everything good in my life had happened through knowing Corinne, which gave her a power over me that, when

I was alone, made me wary. But my wariness melted away again when I saw her.

I would think about asking Corinne to come in, but something always held me back — not shame of her, I told myself, but of my parents and how they might look down on a Negro girl. I told myself that it didn't matter, that Corinne and I still belonged to each other. And while I couldn't see my own future, I was starting to feel that it was out there, waiting for me and Corinne both.

In the meantime, I practised with the cups and balls. The cups themselves, it turned out, weren't gimmicked in any way, but when stacked they nestled together just so, and their rounded rims made it easier to slip a ball underneath. Making a ball jump from underneath one overturned cup to another was easy to do, but longer and more elaborate routines required finger palms, vanishes, holding two balls so they looked like one, fake drops and pickups from a pocket, etc. It was somehow calming to practise these sleights, and I could lose myself for an hour or more. I also worked with handkerchiefs and scarves from my mother's drawer, pieces of rope, metal slugs if I didn't have any coins.

One evening I sat at the dinner table as always while my mother served baked cuttlefish, a dish I hated worse than anything. She served a double portion to Herr Eisler. Miss Kussman began telling some story about an acquaintance who worked in women's clothing at Eaton's and was caught wearing seven pairs of underwear beneath her skirt.

My father, chewing slowly, said to no one in particular, "I have a new job."

My mother stopped serving. "A job? What sort of job?"

"A good one."

"Don't play games, Jacob."

He forked up some potatoes. "I am now an employee of the Might's Directory Company."

"The big telephone book?"

"That is correct. Their office is on Church Street. I had a successful interview. I am now a client information officer. I ask people questions and the answers get printed in the directory." He smiled unpleasantly.

"You go door to door?"

"That's right. Believe me, such a job wasn't easy to get in this day. There were plenty of people ahead of me, educated people. But the man was impressed because of my languages.

Polish, Russian, Yiddish, German, French. A lot of people don't speak English."

"But you don't speak Russian. Or French."

"I can manage well enough," he said with annoyance.

My mother sat down. "That's good, Jacob."

Yes, my father thought, *now she speaks nicely to me.* But he smiled with satisfaction.

24 CLIPBOARD

The city's main rail line ran east-west along the waterfront, but a second track turned upwards to join a third that followed the rise along Dupont Street and then Dundas West. A neighbourhood defined by converging tracks. Small houses stood next to welders' shops, factories making linoleum and pianos, the clanging of the train yard. When the wind turned, the smell from the slaughterhouses was carried in from just north. Here my father had his first assignment. He carried his official Might's Directory Company briefcase, a Kleeman pen in his breast pocket, and a clipboard in his hand holding the printed forms. My mother had mended and brushed his jacket and trousers.

He approached the first house on his list. On the porch was a broken accordion sitting in a galvanized tub with a clothing winger attached to it. He knocked with authority.

"Who is it?"

"A representative of Might's Directory. We require some information for your listing."

The door opened and he saw a woman of middle age in a faded housedress, hair held up by pins. "Do you know my husband, George? George Lafferty?"

My father took the pen from his pocket and wrote down the name. "Occupation?" he asked.

"Do you know where he is? Is he drinking? Can you bring him home?"

"I'm sorry, I don't know. I only take down the information. Is your husband employed?"

"If you find him, tell him to come home. It's been three days."

She closed the door. He heard soft weeping. He thought to knock again, but instead he turned and went back down the steps, catching his trouser leg on a metal screw.

25

AN
ACCUSATION

My aunt was being instructed by the junior minister of the First Presbyterian Church. The minister, a very short Englishman who liked to wear his hair unusually long, complemented Hannah on both her pliancy and her quickness in learning. Hannah herself enjoyed these sessions, for the minister was kind and the need to apply herself gave her a purpose that she hadn't felt in years. It was true that when she wrote to her parents in Otwock, she couldn't get herself to tell them. Instead, she wrote that she was marrying a man named Tov Winkler.

What Hannah hadn't expected was the grief that Hayim was causing her. He was the one who had brought Tobias home, who had encouraged the relationship, who had assured Hannah that there was no disgrace in taking on the faith of her future husband. Yet when he found a small leather-bound copy of the New Testament in the sitting room, he had become mean and sarcastic and she had quickly removed it to her room. Tobias had given her a small gold cross on a chain, but she was careful to keep it under her clothing. Hayim stopped on the way home now to have a drink, and when he came in, he would brandish the newspaper at her and say that she was no better than those criminals in Europe. Then, in the morning, he would apologize, assuring her that he approved of her "new life."

Tobias often stopped in during the evening to see her, and so it was no surprise when he appeared at the door one evening. Hayim had stayed in and they had enjoyed a rare harmonious time, and she told him not to get up from his chair when the bell chimed. But her usual anxious gladness on seeing Tobias gave way to alarm when she saw how agitated he was. He didn't take off his coat but marched straight into the sitting room.

"Toby," said my uncle. "You look like someone who's been robbed. I'll pour you a drink."

"You won't pour me a damn drink. That is exactly what you've been doing all these months. Soothing me, keeping me off guard, lulling me . . ."

"What are you talking about? Hannah, do you know what's going on?"

She could only shake her head, clutching her handkerchief to her lips. She hated male anger and wanted only to hide up in her room while the two of them worked whatever it was out, the way men did. "I will excuse myself," she said.

"No you won't," Tobias said. "The two of you! A conspiracy! That's what it is, a conspiracy."

"Come on, now," said Hayim. "You can't talk this way in my house. Can't you make sense?"

Tobias reached into his jacket, struggled, and at last pulled out an envelope. He smacked it with his other hand as if he were on stage.

"This is what I'm talking about!"

"So, a letter. Let me see it."

Tobias waved it at him without giving it up. "You're trying to take advantage of me, to use my name in order to save your own. But I've caught on to you."

"Tobias," Hannah pleaded. She was already starting to weep. "What is it? This isn't right. It's cruel. Please don't behave this way."

He looked at her, panting heavily. "All right," he said, giving the letter to Hayim. "Go ahead and read it."

Hayim took out the sheet of writing paper and unfolded it. His jaw worked back and forth as he read.

"Tell me what it says, Hayim."

"This isn't for you."

"I'd say it is. Give it to her. I insist."

"If it concerns me, then I want to see it," Hannah said, her voice trembling. He did not prevent her from taking the letter out of his hand.

T. Whitaker,

Are you aware that the woman to whom you are en-gaged has the mark of Satan on her? Surely you don't believe that that orthopaedic shoe hides a natural de-formity. It hides something terrible — a cloven hoof. A foot like that of an animal, like Lucifer himself. If you marry Hannah Kleeman, you marry the devil's whore, sent to lead you to hell.

A Concerned Friend

She could hardly breathe. "What — what is this?"

"I'll tell you what it is," said Hayim. "Some enemy of mine in business. Some envious son of a bitch. Does he think we're living in the Dark Ages? Nobody believes in such nonsense anymore. Toby, you aren't taking this seriously? You should laugh at it. Or be angry at the person who wrote it. You should already have torn it up."

"Of course you think so." He stepped over to Hannah and snatched the letter out of her hands, frightening her. "But I see what you're trying to do, how you want to use me and the name of my family."

"Use you? You forget what your family name is worth these days? The money I loaned you? We bring far more to this marriage than you do."

"I don't understand what I'm hearing," Hannah said.

"The solution is simple," Tobias said, crossing his arms. "All Hannah has to do is remove her shoe and stocking. Then I will see for myself. I should know exactly what I'm marrying."

"Don't insult my sister. I've had enough of this. You're going to have to go."

"No, I'll do it," Hannah said. "Let him see." Immediately, she sat down and began to slip off her shoes. She started rolling down her stockings.

"Hannah, you shouldn't do this. I'm sorry I ever brought Tobias home. Please stop."

But she didn't stop. She presented her naked foot for Tobias to see. She wasn't crying now. Instead, she reached back to undo the button of her dress. She tugged it down, revealing the slip underneath, the straps of her brassiere.

"Hannah! Stop it! Get out of here, Tobias, get out!"

Hayim pushed Tobias towards the door. Hannah stopped undressing and pulled the diamond ring off her finger. She made as if to throw it at Tobias's receding back, but then she changed her mind and closed her fingers around it. It was her ring and she could do what she wanted with it.

26 ISLAND

I t is not boasting to say that the men who hung about the Japanese Magic and Novelty Store said they had never seen a boy learn as quickly as I did. The more I could do, the more generous they became, teaching me what they knew, showing me the secrets of famous apparatus. The card frame. The spirit cabinet. I went to the shop as often as I could, being pulled away only when Corinne enticed me with an invitation to the shed. I could never refuse.

Even when I was out, I practised. With coins, balls, cards, and small gimmicks such as matchboxes or a fake mouse. There was always something moving in my hand. Of course, it wasn't enough to practise by myself, or in front of a mirror. If I saw a kid on the streetcar, holding his mother's hand and staring at me, I would produce the mouse from my pocket or lean over and pull a long ribbon out of his ear. From a couple of old men on a park bench I would borrow a dollar (which took convincing—they always thought I was going to run with it), cause it to disappear, and find it again inside a lemon that I sliced in half with a knife. Once, I entertained four women at a restaurant table through the front window with a small set of linking rings. Even when I didn't want to, when I was too tired or feeling shy, I made myself do it. I practised colour changes, transformations, vanishes—a black spade into a red diamond, a pencil into a cigarette, a rose into smoke.

It was the men who told me about Murenski. A true world-class conjuror who had toured Europe, Russia, Asia, Australia. His name was in the books I had read, with old photographs of a thin, dapper man in top hat and tails. The Great Murenski. Over twenty years ago, while performing in Toronto, his wife had died during the act. He never left the city, becoming a pauper and living in a shack near the cottages on the Island.

The deck vibrated beneath our feet. I had never been on any kind of boat or ferry before and it was thrilling to be moving over water, made even more so by our destination. It was almost dark and the Island only became visible by its scattered lights. They had told me that it was better not to go in the day.

Corinne said, "Are you sure about this Mureeny guy? That he even exists?"

"Murenski."

"And if he does exist, is he going to be glad to see us? I thought those smarty-pants in the magic shop knew everything anyway."

"Nobody knows everything."

"They said he was a hermit."

"Not a hermit. He just likes to keep to himself. On account of his wife dying right here, on the stage of the Royal Alexandra where he was doing a full evening show. It was during the bullet catch."

"The what?"

"Someone fires a gun and the magician catches it on a plate. Or in his hand. Sometimes between his teeth."

"Big surprise she died."

"She didn't die from the trick. A sandbag dropped on her."

The ferry cut its engines and drifted the last few feet into the dock. We waited with the other passengers to disembark, mostly women holding paper bags of groceries, whose families lived year-round in the summer cottages because of the Depression. Corinne followed me along a path covered in overhanging tree branches. We passed cottages with glowing windows. Somebody was stacking a woodpile. Faces under a lantern were eating dinner. Somebody was playing "Happy Days Are Here Again" on a ukulele. We passed the last cottage and passed through another thicket of trees, and then we got to the shore and, again, the dark lake.

I ignored Corinne nagging me to go back. She had always been the brave one, but it was as if she had lost her nerve suddenly. We came to a stand of birches on a crest above the beach. The trees shimmered with flashes of strange light. As we got closer, I saw little fans of tinfoil, made from the liners of cigarette packages, hanging from the branches. A shelter came into view, a patchwork of wooden boards and old doors and crate lids nailed together. The slanted tarpaper roof had a stovepipe sticking up.

"I can't find which door is real," I said.

"Maybe there isn't one."

"Here, this must be it."

I knocked hard, waited, heard something inside, waited some more. At last the door opened—it was slanted and opened at a peculiar angle—and a man stepped out. I had been worried he might be crazy, but he didn't look it. He was tall and frail and neatly dressed in a suit shiny from wear. White hair neatly trimmed and a thin moustache. He looked at us with drooping eyes.

"And whom do I have the pleasure of finding at my door?"

"Mr. Murenski? The Great Murenski?"

"Not so great anymore."

Corinne pointed at me. "He's a magician too."

I blurted out, "I always use the Murenski finish on the rope and ring illusion."

"I'm flattered. I only wish that I still could."

I saw the tremble in his hands. "Did you really know Keller?" I asked.

"So first it's Murenski and now it's Keller?"

"I didn't mean it that way."

"I'm joking. And yes, I knew Keller. He came to spy on my act. Of course, I'd already spied on his."

Corinne said, "He wants you to teach him. He's got money."

"Not a lot of money," I said.

"I don't take money from children. It's getting chilly, isn't it? Would you two mind snitching some wood from the last woodpile you saw? We can get a fire started and make some tea."

It was the beginning of many visits and even more hard work. But he was the real thing, an artist of the conjuring arts. And having a young disciple gave him a new energy for a while, a chance to relive his glory years and see, in my own face, the pleasure and excitement and ambition that he had once had.

27

THE KINDERGARTEN TEACHER

My father did not like having to pay the streetcar fare for work. And too often there were delays—a delivery truck turned over, a horse dead in the street. So he bought a bicycle at a used-furniture dealer on Gerrard Street. It was a black Dawes model that must have been thirty years old. He strapped on his briefcase and began to cycle about the city, knees pointing out awkwardly.

This new job suited my father's temperament. A door would open and in that moment's view—children scrabbling at the table, or a man asleep on the sofa with a hat over his face, or piles of ancient newspapers everywhere—he would get a glimpse of other lives.

It stimulated his imagination and at the same time it was as much information as he wanted.

He had cycled over the Bloor Street viaduct, the green valley and trickling Don River below, and was now working the streets off Pape Avenue. Wroxeter. Frizzell. Dingwall. In an apartment house on Bain, a door was slammed in his face; the man of the house didn't like his wife talking to people. But he had already got what he needed and, standing in the hallway that smelled of boiled eggs, he wrote up the entry on his clipboard. *Morgan, Howard, unemployed. Morgan, Mrs. Frances, attendant, House of Industry.*

At the next apartment, a woman in her undone bathrobe, not trying to seduce him, just not caring if he saw her sagging tits. Next, a husband in an undershirt, the wife out and her sister reading a paperback detective novel.

A man with shaving cream on his face.

A blind man holding a miniature dog.

Elderly twin sisters dressed identically.

He walked outside and sat on the apartment step to eat a sandwich wrapped in wax paper that Bella had made for him. He'd never asked her to, but she'd started leaving a lunch by the door. He ate it as late as possible so as to delay

the pleasure. As he chewed, he amused himself by thinking of the project he had begun to
see in his mind: a miniature clockwork city,
the roofs of the houses tilting back to reveal
the figures moving within — a man tipping
over a table, a child going to the toilet, a couple
moving up and down as they copulated in bed.
He imagined a tavern where two men sprang
punches at one another. A garbage dump where
a boy hit a dog with a stick. Even the mechanical parts he thought through, the little pulleys
and wheels and drives.

With a pocket knife, he peeled the skin
from an apple and ate one thin slice at a time.
Then he brushed himself off and headed into
the next building. It was better maintained,
without the usual pile of undeliverable mail inside the door. He liked to start at the top and
work his way down, and so he climbed the
stairs to the fourth floor.

The first door opened. He saw an unusually
tall woman, glasses, large teeth. "Yes?"

"Excuse me for disturbing you. I am a representative of Might's Directory. You are Mrs.
Goldsmith?"

"The Goldsmiths lived here before me. I'm
Conover. Miss Daphne Conover."

"Are you employed, Miss Conover?"

"I teach kindergarten at Withrow Avenue School. In fact, I've just returned."

"And if I can confirm your telephone number."

"May I ask your name?"

"Kleeman. Jacob Kleeman."

"Like the pen. Mr. Kleeman, do you enjoy games?"

"I don't understand."

"Are you familiar with backgammon?"

"I don't think so."

"It's an ancient game, at least five thousand years old. A board, black and white pieces, dice. You can even bet, although I only play for pennies."

"You don't say."

"I have two cold beers in my icebox. Perhaps you'd care to learn."

"That's very friendly, Miss Conover. And I'm sure it's the best offer I'm going to get today."

He stepped in, looking for a place to put his hat.

THREE

28

ETCHED
GLASS

The thing about magic is that it must be taken very, very seriously. If you don't, it can become a joke. This is why so many performing conjurors have an attitude of pompous gravity on the stage. They are, at heart, deathly afraid of being laughed at. They need to be believed in, like Tinker Bell in the famous play, or they will fade away. Even more, what a conjuror needs is for himself to believe. To believe that what he does has a deeper meaning.

Perhaps this is the most important thing that Murenski taught me in the weeks that I went to see him. But at the time, I was focused far more on the glides, shifts, and palms, the methods of misdirection, the uses of silk thread, secret pockets, black velvet, small mirrors. Every hour spent with Murenski meant days of intense practice afterwards. I had the natural yearning of the young and also the unexplainable confidence of someone who believed he was born with a divine gift. Still, I didn't think I was ready. I'm not sure that I would ever have felt myself ready without Corinne's big hands shoving me from behind. Shoving me right up to the frosted glass door with the letters etched into it. *Moses Ludwig, Manager.* It was my fault for telling her that the Brant didn't have a magician on the card anymore.

Through the floor, I could feel the vibration from the theatre below. I touched my hand to the door.

"Come on, big shot," Corinne said. "Knock louder. Houdini could walk straight through that door."

"Houdini was an escape artist." I knocked louder.

"Who the hell is it?"

I opened the door. The man behind the desk was eating a pastrami sandwich with both hands. Jowly, with heavy-lidded eyes, wheezing between chews. The sort of man who would play a theatre manager in the movies.

"If you want free tickets, you can scram. I don't care if your ma's a cripple or your old man is on the dole. Those cheapskates across the street never put on enough mustard. Get out of here, kids."

"Mr. Ludwig," I said. "I want to audition."

"I guess you're trying to make me laugh till I die."

"He's serious," Corinne said.

"You two do a midget version of *Uncle Tom's Cabin*? I can get plenty of midgets if I want them, and believe me I don't."

"Maybe I could leave you my card," I said. I reached into my cotton jacket and pulled out a dove. Its head hung limp. "I think I suffocated it."

"That's an original touch. Jesus, an animal-killing act."

The bird shuddered, shook itself, and flapped upright onto my finger. "Are you all right?" I said. I threw the bird up into the air, only for it to become a shower of confetti.

"Hey, you're making a mess in here." Mr. Ludwig brushed the paper bits off his sandwich. "What else can you do?"

"Mr. Ludwig," I said, tugging at one sleeve to show nothing was hidden under my shirt cuff, and then the other. From the folds at my elbow I palmed a hidden roll of bills that I now fanned out with my fingers. "What I can do is make you money."

The man half snorted, half chuckled. "I doubt it. But I'm the easiest mark in the world. A kid magician might be novel for a couple of weeks. Even if you screw up, you might get their sympathy. Can you do eight minutes?"

"Sure."

"I've got to figure out some way to bill you. Youngest member of the Magic Circle in London, Blackstone's illegitimate kid, something like that. You'll work every night but Sunday, plus Saturday afternoons, ten bucks a week."

"That isn't much," Corinne said.

"He isn't much either. Listen, we're the last straight vaudeville house in town. Every other one is showing movies for half the night if it hasn't closed down. Here are the rules: Late for one show and you lose a day's pay. Show up intoxicated and you're suspended. Complaints from any of the girls and you're out. Bomb and you're out. I get in a bad mood and you're out. You can start two weeks from Thursday."

"Thanks, Mr. Ludwig."

"I'm going to need a letter from your parents. That they're okay with this."

"I'm an orphan."

"That's my good luck. What's your name, anyway?"

"Benjamin Kleeman."

"We need one of those magician names for you. The Great Kidini. Nah. The Little Wonder. That might do. Listen, Benjamin. You want to get in my good books? Run across to the deli and get me some more mustard in a paper cup."

The phone rang. I hurried out of the office, closing the door behind me. Corinne gave a little shriek. I felt the blood drain from my body. I had tricks, but I didn't have an act, not even eight minutes.

29

TOSCA

Daphne Conover, the woman who taught my father the game of backgammon, was the oldest daughter of a Methodist minister from Bracebridge. She was thirty-seven years old and had turned down a proposal of marriage when she was nineteen. Even then she knew that men did not attract her, that she did not want children of her own, that she was destined for university and a career. She had a woman friend, a private school teacher named Elspeth Watson, with whom she spent every Friday and Saturday evening.

My father, it turned out, was good company. He could be quite cynical and witty. He told her stories about the people he met during the day. He did not appear to want any sexual favours from her. Best of all, he was an excellent backgammon player. She would put *Tosca* or *Rigoletto* on the record player and they would drink beer and play.

For his part, my father enjoyed Daphne's company. He found himself more talkative than he had been in years. Backgammon intrigued him from the beginning, and soon became a passion. It was the only game he never tried to cheat at. He puzzled over the patterns and strategies of a game so simple and yet with such depth.

At home, his spirit was lighter. He found himself more kindly disposed towards my mother and me. In his free time he began to work on the house, stripping off the old wallpaper, caulking the drafty windows.

This reformed behaviour made my mother happier but also more guilt-ridden. She was having sex with the emotionally wrought Sigismond several times a week, usually in the morning before opening up the stand. She worried that Jacob suspected. In fact, my father still had not the slightest idea. She worried about me too, with more reason.

30 TRICKS

The act that I came up with was really just a series of unconnected tricks. First some colour changes with scarves, then vanishing a dove, then the lota bowls—three brass bowls emptied of water to the last drop that became full again. It was a simple trick, one only had to put a finger over a hole under the rim of the bowl, but it had to be done slowly and with a sort of hushed reverence. I finished with a cup and balls routine.

I also worked out my patter, but the words came out stiffly and if anything took away from the tricks. "I will now make this dove vanish," I would say, giving away the effect.

Practising so hard, and being so afraid, I

didn't have a lot of time for Corinne. I thought this was what a woman did, wait for you. I didn't see that she had ambitions of her own, even if she was less sure of where they might take her and was more realistic about the obstacles.

Of course, she came to my first performance. Corinne was the only one who knew besides Murenski, who never left the Island. The master of ceremonies came out and made some jokes and then began to introduce me. He said that I wasn't called the Little Wonder for the reason the audience thought. "You have such dirty minds." For some reason the small band in the pit played "Jeanie with the Light Brown Hair" as I came onstage. The lights were hot and blinding and I couldn't see the audience scattered in the seats near the front and up in the balcony. I tried to speak, but my throat felt closed up and I couldn't get any words out. So I started anyway, pulling a red scarf out of the air. The scarf tricks went well enough, but I tried to be too careful with the dove, not wanting to hurt it, and I could tell by the titters that some people in front saw me change it for a dummy before collapsing the cage.

I carried out the table for the cups and balls.

It hadn't occurred to me that the act was too intimate for a large theatre until someone in the balcony shouted, *"What are you doing down there, counting rice? We can't see!"* But I kept going through the routine to the end, when the curtain closed and the band played "Oh! Susanna."

31

ALBUM

I hadn't gone to see my aunt Hannah for a long while, as I had better things to do these days. And besides, I was making money now and felt less need for the handful of dollars she always slipped me when I was leaving. But I knew of her failed engagement and for some time I had been worried about her, for she seemed the most delicate person I knew. So I went in the late afternoon, when I knew that Uncle Hayim would be at the factory. And besides, a few extra dollars wouldn't hurt.

The maid knew me by now and ushered me into the sitting room, where Hannah was looking through a leather-covered album of photographs. "Come and see," she said, patting the space beside her. "These are your relatives too."

She showed me my grandparents. My grandfather was grim-looking, with a wide face and a heavy beard and deep lines about his eyes. He wore the traditional Orthodox garb, dark and heavy, with a bowler hat. My grandmother was a thickset peasant of a woman, squat and sturdy, beefy arms crossed, a kerchief on her head. Hannah spoke warmly of them both, her eyes becoming damp, but I couldn't connect her words to the photograph.

I saw aunts and uncles and cousins grouped around a table brimming with dishes of food. The shot had been taken by one of my cousins, who ran a photography business. He had taken formal portraits too, using a draped background painted like a Greek temple. Here was a teenage girl playing the violin, a small boy holding a prayer book, a young man in some sort of uniform. For each one Hannah told me the name, how old he or she was, and what she knew about the person from letters she received every week. I saw the front of the family hotel, which looked smaller than I had imagined, the plaster front chipped in several places, beside the entrance a three-wheeled cart with the name of the hotel in Hebrew letters.

Hannah must have seen these photographs many times, but she looked at them again, thrilled to have someone to share them with. She told me that her father's — my grandfather's — letters had grown increasingly anguished and then had stopped. Another relative wrote to say that he'd fallen ill and had taken to his bed.

"I would do anything to see them," she said. I nodded, although I couldn't imagine anything that I'd rather do less. I looked at my aunt, at the intense light in her eyes. After all these years, she still belonged more to that world than to this one.

32

BIG ILLUSION

I did not let the stagehands carry my black art table or other props, but carried them myself off the stage and into the wings. An act called the Five Trelawny Sisters was on next. Only two of them were actually sisters. The older one never failed to find it amusing to rub her sequined breasts against me as she passed, assuming I was as innocent as I looked.

My act had grown to twelve minutes. The scarf routine was more elaborate and now I produced three doves, which I otherwise kept in a cage in the backyard, having told my mother that I was raising them for money. I found a way to sell the cups and balls to the upper balcony, by moving downstage and using larger motions. I added the black art table, on which I grew flowers in a vase and then made the vase disappear, and a spirit slate where answers to questions from the audience appeared. I talked when I had to but otherwise kept my mouth shut. None of it was original and it would still be a long time before I had much stage presence and was able to make the audience believe they were part of something extraordinary. But I was getting better.

"Hey, kid, Mr. Ludwig wants to see you." The stage manager pointed his thumb over his shoulder. It wasn't payday and I hadn't messed up tonight, so I could not guess what Mr. Ludwig wanted. He had fired a comedy team and a girl singer to save money, so maybe it was my turn. I hadn't really expected to last this long.

The office door was open and Mr. Ludwig waved me in. "Come in, Ben, and close the door. Don't look so spooked. Let's talk a minute. How are you enjoying your spot?"

"I like it."

"Good. You're improving fast. The audience likes your fresh face. But I think it works better when you don't say anything. Until you talk, half the people think you're mute. I'm considering moving you to a better spot, just before the second intermission. You think you can get them to return to their seats?"

"Sure I can, Mr. Ludwig."

"That's the stuff. I've been thinking about you, Ben. I'd like to show an interest. You've got natural talent, still a little crude but coming along. And there's something else you've got, something in your eyes that puts the audience on your side. Maybe we've got a chance at making something here. A strong act that might get you on what's left of the circuit. Not just here but Montreal, Boston, Philadelphia, Chicago. Even New York."

"I want that, Mr. Ludwig."

"There are two things you need, Ben. One is a manager who will go to bat for you like a son of a bitch. That's me. The other thing is something new in your act. A showstopper."

"A big illusion, you mean?"

"That's it. Not scarves or cards or balls or any of that stuff. A routine that fills the stage, that's a real drama. A story that keeps them on the edge of their seats."

"Like Carter used to have. And Horace Goldin."

"You got it. Only more up to date. Now, I can come up with the story. But we need that big illusion. Have you got one?"

"Well, I know of one. A really good one. But I'm going to need something."

"What's that?"

"A lion."

"You're pulling my leg."

"A real lion. With a big mane. The more fierce-looking, the better."

"Even supposing I could find one, it wouldn't be cheap. And there's the upkeep. I'd have to believe you're a good investment."

"I am a good investment, Mr. Ludwig."

He leaned over the desk and stared into my eyes. I made myself look back and not even blink. He sat back again, grabbing a cigar and a lighter. "I get a certain feeling in my stomach," he said, striking a flame, "when I'm right about something."

33

ROASTED CHICKEN

I knew what happened in the illusion, but I didn't know how it was done. So Corinne and I went to Wasserman's Poultry Shop in the market and I picked out a good chicken from the cages. Mr. Wasserman killed it himself and his wife plucked and gutted it before tying it up in brown paper.

We took the ferry to the Island and presented the chicken to Murenski. He had a homemade spit over his fire and we turned the chicken, dripping fat crackling on the hot coals. The smell brought stray dogs into the surrounding trees. Murenski drew it off the spit, cut it into pieces, and fished some potatoes out of the coals. My lips burned from the hot skin of the chicken.

"It isn't an illusion for someone without experience." He took a bite of chicken and then a swallow from a brown bottle. "For me to explain it is nothing. I can draw precise sketches of the apparatus. But performing it isn't about nimble hands. It takes speed, strength, and confidence. It's not a trick for a boy, even a talented one. And then of course there's the animal. It has to be used to performing."

"Can't he use a fake lion?" Corinne asked. "Stuffed maybe?"

"Ralph Gelden tried that once. He got laughed out of the theatre."

I said, "I've brought paper and a ruler and a pencil. For you to do the sketches."

Murenski sighed. "May I at least finish my supper?"

Corinne's mouth shone with chicken grease. She said, "I don't understand you magicians. Why you enjoy tricking people."

"It isn't tricking people," I said. "I don't know what it is exactly. Making people see something they've never seen before."

"But they want to see it," Murenski added.

"Not just see it," I said. "Believe in it."

Corinne shook her head. "I don't know what you two are talking about."

I still didn't absolutely know myself. We finished eating, and then Murenski made the sketches, drawing the cage from various angles, explaining to me how it worked and what problems to look out for. He had trouble getting the lines straight because of his tremor. When we were done, he shook both my and Corinne's hands. "I think you should put these drawings away for a few years," he said. "But I don't think you will."

We took the ferry back. Corinne said that her aunt and uncle had gone to Buffalo for two days to visit relatives. She was supposed to be staying with neighbours, only she had neglected to tell them and so had the house to herself. We could be in a real bed for the first time.

My plans for Corinne and myself were firming up, even if I wasn't ready to share them with her. The two of us married and with beautiful coffee-skin children living in a fine city house, and my name and image on tall posters outside the theatre where I was performing each night to packed crowds. We walked to her uncle's and, just as she said, the lights were off and it looked deserted. Happily, she pulled me up the steps to the front door, taking out a key that she kept on a string around her neck. But she frowned on finding the door unlocked, and when we went in, there was a figure standing in the dark.

"Daddy?"

"Corinne, honey. You never seem to expect me."

He turned on the lamp and I saw her father in his Pullman porter uniform, cap laid on the table. Corinne went up and kissed him on the cheek. "What are you doing home?"

"I do get to come home sometimes," he said. "And I have some news. Where's your aunt and uncle?"

"Visiting Louis in Buffalo."

"They left you all on your own?"

"I'm supposed to be staying next door. I just haven't gone over yet."

"I bet. And your friend — Benjamin, I believe — he's going too? I don't like you pulling the wool over your aunt and uncle's eyes. Now I think it's time to say good night to Benjamin."

"But what's the news, Daddy?"

"We're going to be moving, Corinne."

"Again?"

"The company wants me stationed in Chicago. I'll be able to come home more often. You'll like Chicago. It's a big city and there are a lot of coloured people there."

"But Daddy —"

"I'm tired, daughter. I've been on my feet for fourteen hours. We need to turn in. Can you get home all right, Benjamin?"

"Yes, sir."

"You better be off, then."

All the way home, I thought about this problem of Corinne having to move to Chicago. Her father struck me as a reasonable man. He would learn to accept me if he saw that I was necessary for Corinne's happiness. I took a bunch of quarters out of my pocket to practise while I walked. Never think you're so good that your skills can't get any better. Murenski taught me that.

34 STINK

The lion came from a travelling circus marooned in Ithaca, New York. The city council had taken extraordinary measures, sending five police officers, to prevent the owner's departure until some four dozen bills were paid to local businesses. The lion was an elderly male, half toothless and ratty-maned, that had been mauled by a new and bigger male so that it now refused to perform with the other lions. "Gentle and dumb," the circus owner had assured Mr. Ludwig. Mr. Ludwig hired a horse trainer to take care of it in an empty warehouse at the foot of Frederick Street.

Corinne and I went to visit it because, Corinne said, the lion and I needed to become friends. We didn't talk about what her father had said. I didn't know what Corinne was thinking, whether she wanted to go to Chicago or whether the thought of leaving me was too unbearable. I wanted it to be unbearable. She was sixteen and I figured could make her own decisions if she wanted to. I just didn't know if she wanted to.

The horse trainer came twice a day to feed it and muck out the cage, which could be divided in half. Most of the time it was alone in the dark. When we came in, the lion was usually lying flat on its stomach. It would open its eyes and look at us. Corinne would push me to the bars, telling me to coo to the thing and throw it treats — chicken heads that we got for nothing in the market. It sure was big, saliva dripping from the corner of its droopy mouth, and all it did with the chicken head was stare at it.

"I feel sorry for him," Corinne said.

I answered, "I'm worrying more about me at the moment."

The lion yawned. I could smell the stink of its breath.

Mr. Ludwig had his stagehands build the set and the equipment. It took two weeks. He had the whole act worked out. Several of the other performers had to be offered bonuses to participate, and I had to cut out of school for several afternoons in order to rehearse. We did everything exactly as we would in performance, except that we didn't use the lion. Mr. Ludwig didn't want the expense of moving him back and forth until the actual shows began and some money was coming in. Anyway, there wasn't anything for the lion to learn. It was going to be like the lady who gets sawed in half and has to just lie there.

At the rehearsals, the other actors complained of my wooden style, but otherwise things seemed to go all right. But I felt as if all of this had happened far too quickly, that it hadn't been long ago that I was trying to keep Corinne from noticing a coin in my hand. I began waking in the night from recurring dreams of drowning.

35

HANDBILL

Mr. Ludwig had two thousand handbills printed up. I left one with a ticket for my mother at her stall in the market. Another for my father in the drawer where he kept his shirts. I left handbills and tickets for Corinne and her father, for my aunt, for Miss Pensler, even for Herr Eisler. I left one in the mailbox for my uncle Hayim. I took the ferry to hand one to Murenski, even though I knew he wouldn't leave the Island.

"In India," Murenski said, "I learned the secret of out-of-body travel. So I do plan to send my spiritual essence."

"Sure," I said. "And I really am the saviour of the Hebrews."

"Yes, you are." Murenski pointed to the handbill. "Twice an evening, four times on Saturday."

36

CROSSING

O nce she calmed down and began to feel like herself again, my aunt Hannah was glad that she was not going to marry Tobias Whitaker. The memory of trying to take off her clothes didn't fill her with the slightest shame. But the effect was to make her see how small her life was, how unconnected to anything or anyone that mattered.

Without her lessons to occupy her, she found herself thinking constantly of her family in Otwock—her mother and father, her aunts and uncles, her growing cousins. She always believed that someday she would see them again, and now, the letters said, her father was bedridden and hardly spoke. He had to be fed with a spoon. Two of her more adventurous cousins had decided to leave the country in the hope of getting out of Europe, but their whereabouts were unknown.

When I came to visit, she asked for my help. She opened a cotton handkerchief to show the diamond ring inside. Where could she sell it? she wanted to know. I did not let her go to a pawnshop but took her to Scheuer's, the diamond merchants on lower Yonge Street. These days there were too many people selling and not enough buying, but it was a good diamond, and after I told the man with the glass in his eye that we would take it somewhere else, she got a decent price.

I was not with her after that, when she took a cab to the shipping office on Toronto Street and bought a train ticket to Montreal and passage to Antwerp for two days later. Hayim would be in Montreal on business. She went into the Imperial Bank and withdrew the rest of what her brother had deposited into her account. At home, she packed two large trunks, all the clothes she had, so that she might share them with the others.

The crossing would be difficult, as would the train and then the wagon to Otwock. But she would kiss her mother again. She would stroke her father's gaunt cheek. She would be with them, whatever might happen.

37

FIRST NIGHT

Moses Ludwig said that he was trying to cash in on vaudeville before it took its last wheezy breaths, but I didn't believe it. It could not possibly be dying the moment I arrived. I volunteered to change the three or four bulbs burned out in the marquee. The woman who sold tickets held the ladder.

The handbills and some small newspaper advertisements did result in a larger house than usual for the first Friday night show. Single men who didn't want to return to their fleabag rooms, women in pairs or with their whining children, couples out for a lark.

Sigismond Eisler arrived twenty-five minutes before the first act. What did the boy mean, he thought, inviting him to the theatre? In Germany, he had gone to see the Berlin Modern Art Ensemble perform *Woyzeck*. He was not interested in clowns in slouch hats slapping one another. Nevertheless, he was here, perhaps because the boy reminded him of his own child. He purchased a bag of peanuts and tried to tip the usher a nickel as was done back home, but the surprised young man dropped the coin.

Miss Pensler came in next, male heads turning to look, alerted by her unusual height. She took a seat on the aisle, removed her hat, and took from her purse a traveller's edition of the poems of Thomas Hardy.

My mother paused to let another, pushier woman enter first. She sniffed, detecting mildew, then chose a seat near the back, under the overhang of the balcony.

Corinne came in accompanied by her father. He wore a neat suit and tie and a new fedora. Negroes were not required to go up to the balcony, but her father believed it best to do so and they took seats by the rail. Their possessions had already been sent ahead. They had only small bags for the train trip to Chicago, which her father had left in the porters' lockers at Union Station along with his uniform. They would walk to the station as soon as the show was over. Corinne had told me that when the curtain came down she would run from her father, who would never be able to keep up, and that she would hide until he was forced to go to the station without her for fear of missing the train. He'd never missed a train in nineteen years. Once he was gone, he would have to agree to her staying with her aunt and uncle.

My uncle Hayim stayed home. He could not get over his sister's return to the old country. He sat in his shirt sleeves, a bottle of Seagram's at his elbow, and he would spend the night in that chair.

The house lights dimmed. My father groped his way to a seat.

The opening act was a plate spinner, followed by a fake Siamese-twin comedy routine, a Shirley Temple look-alike, and a parrot act. The curtain closed for several minutes while the band played. A spotlight came on and the music turned ominous. The curtain pulled away to show the German chancellor, Adolf Hitler, complete with swept hair and little moustache, uniform and boots, pacing back and forth before a trembling staff under a military tent.

I watched from the wings. The actor's gestures and strut looked just like the newsreels. He ranted about his scheme to conquer the world. The dialogue had been written by someone named Freddy Katz, a Broadway rewrite man who owed Mr. Ludwig a favour. It didn't matter how stiff and melodramatic the lines were, that actor was genuinely scary to watch.

The Jews, Hitler said, would come first. They would be easy to defeat, for they were a corrupt and unmanly race. A general stepped forward. Yes, *Mein Herr*, he said. Easy except for one thing. A Hebrew boy who lived among the poor. A deaf-mute. What possible trouble could such a boy cause? Hitler asked. This boy, said the general, was said to be a wonder-worker, a maker of miracles.

Nonsense! Hitler became furious. He cracked his riding crop over the general's back. I knew that the actor's coat was padded, but still I flinched. This boy, Hitler said, must be captured at once. We shall go to the ghetto of the Jews.

The curtain came down. The tent was pulled up into the flies and the stagehands hurried to set up the ghetto. I adjusted my cap and checked my pockets again. An actor in rags got behind a plywood cart as the curtain went up. From the pit came the plaintive strains of a violin. Four peasant Jews rushed onto the stage screaming for help. My heart started to race. In the arms of one, a young girl hung limp. She was the Shirley Temple look-alike, but without her curly wig, legs bare and face dirty; somehow she had become this other child. The mother cried that her daughter had fallen into the well. She had lain under the water for many minutes. They laid her carefully on the ground. Another listened to her breast. No heartbeat, she said. No breath, said someone else. The mother began a terrible wailing.

"The boy! Call the boy who works wonders!"

Two peasants ran back into the wings and grabbed me by the arms. "Keep your focus," one hissed. And then they were taking me downstage.

I didn't want to think about the people in the audience, so I looked down at the girl. At rehearsals she'd always squirmed and complained, but now she lay absolutely still. I was almost afraid that she really had stopped breathing. I knelt down, put my hand delicately to her mouth, and slowly drew from between her lips a blue ribbon, as if it were the water in her lungs. I drew out more and more, many feet of ribbon, until the end appeared. A peasant knelt down to listen. Still she doesn't breathe. I motioned for her to be laid atop the cart. Then I took the mother's shawl, stretching it out in front of the girl. I let it fall upon her shape as if it were a shroud. The mother began to sob quietly. I held out my hand to stay her. I concentrated on the shrouded form and reached out my hands towards it.

The girl's shawl-covered body began to rise. It rose until it hovered just above our heads. The peasants onstage gasped, cried, reached out to touch the frills of the shawl. I motioned for them to step back. I reached up, grasped a corner of the shawl, and pulled it sharply away. Nothing. The girl had vanished.

Where had the child gone? I looked at an old man and gestured to him. The old man said, "We must put our trust in the God who made us His chosen people." I waved the shawl in the air and let it settle onto the ground. I pinched it at the centre and slowly pulled it up. As it rose, the shawl took on the shape of a figure, making the audience gasp. I pulled it away to reveal the young girl, her eyes closed. She wavered as if about to fall, but a peasant caught her. The girl opened her eyes. She looked about as if waking from a dream.

"Mamma?"

The mother rushed to take the girl in her arms. Everyone laughed, cried, spoke to one another, danced about. Only I remained still. And then the musicians struck up a military march. Two Nazis goose-stepped onto the stage, followed by Hitler himself. And behind him, four more soldiers pulled an iron cage on wheels. Inside the cage, the lion paced and turned and even roared. The audience's excited reaction rose above the music. Hitler came right up to me, and when he spoke, his spittle hit my face. "Hold this boy!"

Two solders grabbed me and I pretended to struggle. Meanwhile, two others dropped a big sheet over the top of the cage, covering the side facing the audience. The sheet had a large red swastika on it. The soldiers dragged me up to the cage. One reached for the latch on the door, but I could still see the lion, its eyes fearful even as it roared again. An actor behind hit the lever, secretly tipping the floor and causing the startled lion to slide into the hidden

compartment. Up came my costume from below, along with a dummy of me.

The soldiers made a big show of throwing
me into the cage and shutting the door.

Did I hear my mother cry out, or was that
somebody else? Quickly I pulled on the lion
costume, legs first, then arms and head, pulling up the inside zipper. It was heavily padded
and reinforced to make me look much larger.
The realism was good enough to briefly fool an
audience that had already seen a real lion and
believed it still to be there. I kept hunched over
the bloody dummy of myself while the stage
lights, already dim, flashed blue and red.

I heard Hitler shout the cue for the sheet to
be pulled away from the cage. As it came up, I
made as if I were disembowelling the dummy,
moving as viciously as I could. I threw myself
onto the cage door, bringing it crashing down.
The impact on my hands and knees made me
yelp with pain. The audience screamed while
Hitler too cried out in terror and fled the stage,
even as I yanked off the lion's head and revealed
the boy underneath.

38
RAIN

My mother, Bella Kleeman, threw open the door of the theatre and walked furiously up Yonge Street. A light rain fell. What she would do with her son when he came home! When had all this happened? What sort of people was he associating with? Really, she was the one who ought to be smacked, lost in her own suffering and pleasure. How had she missed the end of his childhood?

Sigismond Eisler saw her leave. He wanted to catch up but thought better of it and stooped to tie his shoe. He wondered if he and Bella were over. Outside, he pulled his hat low to keep the rain out of his eyes. It had been nine weeks since he had heard from his wife and child. His eyes filled. Maybe they were in hiding somewhere in the countryside. Maybe they were still safe.

This is what my father thought: *My son has turned out to be clever.* He didn't get up from his seat but remained as the band played and a dancing couple came on. So he had passed something on to the boy.

A passing automobile threw up a sluice of dirty water that soaked the hem of Miss Pensler's dress. She felt a glow of pride for the boy who had come to her wanting a book. Getting into a cab, she opened her purse and fished out a pack of Buckinghams. For a reason she couldn't fathom, she thought of her father, who had been hit by a delivery truck in front of the Telegram building when she was five years old. The match flared and she drew on the cigarette. She could remember only one image of him, standing in his undershirt in the kitchen, peeling an apple.

Corinne's father held her arm tightly. He walked her to the front of the theatre, but she stopped and asked if he would wait a minute for her. He looked hard at her and then he said all right. Corinne hurried back inside. She went up to the ticket booth, politely asked for a sheet of paper and a pen, and then wrote a single line. She folded the paper and wrote *To Benjamin Kleeman* on it before giving it to the ticket seller. Then she went back to her father and the two of them walked quickly down to the station. Her father had just enough time to change into his uniform before they boarded.

39

ESSENTIALS

The lion had died while confined in the hidden space under the cage floor. It couldn't have suffocated as the compartment was properly ventilated. Nor were there any signs of injury. Likely it had died of a heart attack.

"Without a lion, we don't have an act," said Moses Ludwig in his office. "I don't know where to get another one. Besides, he was eating me out of house and home. I've already put a lot of dough into this. And if there's a war? Actually, I should say *when* there's a war."

"But the act worked," I said. "The audience—did you hear them?"

"I hate to tell you this. There's a magician I know, working the circuit already. He's willing to buy the act from me—cage, set, costume, script, the works. I'll break even. Next month we're going to start showing pictures. Sorry, Benjamin, it's just the way things are."

I didn't say anything. In my hand was Corinne's note. I had already read it, but I hadn't taken it in, not really. I put on my jacket and knapsack and closed the door behind me. I went down the back stairs and out into the lane behind the theatre. The ground was slick and caught the reflection of the light over the door. The actor who played Hitler hurried past me. I couldn't go back to my parents' house, not with Corinne gone and not without performing to look forward to. In my knapsack I had a marked deck, my chop cups, a few essentials.

I hunched my shoulders in the damp air. Magic could make people forget whatever they needed to forget for a little while, and that was it. I knew there were bigger things going on out there, catastrophes awaiting, but none of it meant anything to me right now. I planned to write my parents a letter when I got a chance, just so they'd know I wasn't dead.

40 FLIGHT

When my father got home, he did not look for my mother but instead went straight to my room. He turned on the light, but even as the bulb flickered on, it made a popping sound and went out. In the gloom, he moved over to the dresser where he could see the shapes of the mechanical toys he had made so long ago — monkey, fish, crocodile, lion, bird. He picked up the key, put it between his teeth, and lifted the large bird with both hands. He carried it to the open window.

He had to put the bird down on the bed to haul up the window. The rain had stopped. Carefully, he wound up the spring mechanism, keeping one hand over its back so that the wings couldn't move. They pushed against his fingers, not with the frantic energy of a real bird, but with the steady and insistent pressure of a machine. He had never wanted to risk trying it out so that he might continue to hold on to the possibility of it actually working. But now he held it out as a pigeon fancier might hold one of his racers and awkwardly shoved his arms through the open window as he let go.

The bird flapped hard. Laboriously. The body dipped downwards, but the wingbeat levelled it and the second caused it to thrust forward as if it were paddling through water. The mechanical whirr was as loud as a dozen cicadas. The wing flaps steadied as it rose and, wheeling, just missed the chimney of the house across the street.

It flew on. Over streets, over the buildings of the university with the zigzag pattern on their roofs, over the playing fields towards the downtown. Anyone seeing it from below would have thought it some large bird of prey, sick or wounded, struggling up through the air. It rose higher still, over businesses and shops, over Brant's Vaudeville, over church spires. It gazed down with its glass eye, and then its beak opened and it gave out a single rasping call.

ACKNOWLEDGEMENTS

Many thanks to everyone at Anansi, especially Melanie Little for presenting the manuscript in the best light, Jared Bland and Sarah MacLachlan for their enthusiasm and editing skills, and Janice Zawerbny for seeing it through to the end. Once again Rebecca Comay and Bernard Kelly gave first readings and offered valuable suggestions. Patrick Crean has been very supportive of my recent work, and gracious as well. And a final but most necessary acknowledgement and thanks to Marc Côté.

Grants from the Canada Council and Ontario Arts Council gave me the necessary time.

ABOUT THE AUTHOR

Cary Fagan is an award-winning author who is known for timeless stories that reveal complex and universal themes. He has written several novels, including *Valentine's Fall*, which was a finalist for the Toronto Book Award, *The Mermaid of Paris*, *Felix Roth*, as well as several books for children. He has been an editor and contributor to several magazines and newspapers, including the *Globe and Mail* and the *Montreal Gazette*. His books have been published in the U.S., Canada, and Germany. He was the winner of the Jewish Book Committee Prize for Fiction, and most recently, his collection of short stories, *My Life Among the Apes*, was longlisted for the Scotiabank Giller Prize.